THE
BIRTHDAY
WEEKEND

BOOKS BY LESLEY SANDERSON

THE
BIRTHDAY
WEEKEND

LESLEY SANDERSON

Bookouture

Published by Bookouture in 2020

An imprint of Storyfire Ltd.
Carmelite House
50 Victoria Embankment
London EC4Y 0DZ

www.bookouture.com

ISBN: 978-1-80019-079-5
eBook ISBN: 978-1-80019-078-8

To Alison, Kay, Anne, Richard S, Sandra and Trudy, for happy memories of Cryfield Halls all those years ago.

PROLOGUE

She fooled us all, that first time. One look and I knew. Why was I the only one who could see through her? It was all pretence. I could see the darkness underneath that girlish exterior. She made her feelings known and turned us all against one another. She played us like spinning tops, whirling around, unable to stop, and when she wanted to finish the game, it was too late. I'd spun out of control and there was no going back.

CHAPTER ONE

Amy's message arrives during netball practice. I take aim and the ball sails through the net. I punch the air, high-five Mel, my heart pumping. The ball goes back to centre and my watch buzzes with a text. A quick scroll up and I see the word *invitation*. My heart pumps even harder. Finally. What has she decided? I turn my attention back to the game, dodge behind the goalkeeper and run across the court to catch the ball. Aim, shoot, goal. We win three-nil.

For once I don't go to the pub afterwards, the team's usual weekly tradition. No laughing and dissecting the game with my team-mates – my friends – over a pint or two. I want to get home to my flat, to *our* flat, that one small word sending a thrill down my spine. Never will I take Theo for granted again. Everything feels new with him; we're tiptoeing our way along the path, baby steps, both determined to make it work this time.

My thoughts turn to Amy's message. Birthdays are a Big Thing for Amy, always have been. Celebrations are spread over at least a week; her twenty-first set a record by lasting three weeks, and included a trip away, a meal, a club night and an all-night pub crawl. In two weeks' time it will be her thirty-fifth – not normally a milestone, but after the year she's had, she deserves to celebrate.

Theo won't be home for at least half an hour, and I stick a vegetable lasagne I made before I went out to netball in the oven. Once I'm sitting at the kitchen table with a mug of tea in front of me, I locate Amy's message. *Invitation* surely means a party – it's been a while since I had a good dance. These days I prefer to curl up on the sofa with a book, or go out for a glass of wine with a close friend, checking in on our emotions and putting the world to rights.

I've finally decided what I'm doing for The Birthday. I've set up a WhatsApp group – see you in there!

Oh, Amy – as if I didn't have enough WhatsApp groups to be part of. I open the link inviting me to the group entitled *Amy's Birthday*, wondering how many messages I'm going to be bombarded with. Amy will kill me if I fail to join, so I click on accept. No doubt she's hired a huge venue and invited her vast menagerie of family and friends.

I sip my tea and frown when I see the other members of the group. That can't be right. It's tiny, four in total. Maybe this is a subgroup, her close friends who she wants to help her organise the event. There have to be more people invited somewhere else; perhaps that's a separate group. *Who am I trying to kid?* I close my eyes and take a deep breath, realising what Amy has done. It's a reunion. It's *the* reunion.

I go back to the group. Four names, the other three as familiar to me as my own. Close friends throughout three years at university. Some experiences bring you closer. When our world collapsed, we clung to one another for survival – at first. Until it broke us.

I read the list aloud.

'Amy Barnes, Kat Carr, Louise Redfern, Daisy Tannet.'

Amy tried so hard to keep us together. The four of us met in our first year at Buckinghamshire University, graduating almost fifteen years ago. How time flies. Graduation took place during a difficult time for us, and if it wasn't for Amy, I'm sure we'd have gone our separate ways. Exactly a year later, she arranged for us all to meet up for a lunch in London, a tiny bistro in Covent Garden, followed by a browse around the craft market.

Over lunch, I looked at these three women, all of whom had confided their darkest fears to me, and was overcome by waves of sadness. Conversation was stilted, fixing on safe topics, nothing of consequence, as we all avoided the subject that was really bothering us. Daisy and Kat made their excuses before we'd even got around to coffee. Undeterred, Amy suggested we make it an annual reunion, but somehow it never happened: one of us was always busy, another away, so many excuses on offer.

Amy is like a spider at the centre of her web, keeping us all linked together, although the threads have loosened and split over the years. She keeps us updated with each other's news, so we're kind of in the loop together. Five years ago, Kat moved to London, so the two of us have seen each other quite a lot lately, recent events bringing us closer together.

My voice falters on Daisy's name, a bubble of complicated feelings rising inside me. We've had more contact over the last couple of years, since Amy's diagnosis, but a blush comes to my cheeks whenever I recall the last time we saw each other, well over a year ago now. Loyalty in friendship is a trait I pride myself on; any knots in my relationships have to be unpicked, no matter how long it takes. Daisy's knot is proving hard to unravel, but she, out of the four of us, should know how loyal I can be.

It's obvious what Amy is doing. Her illness has caused her to re-evaluate everything in her life, and one thing she hates more than anything is disharmony. She knows me too well – springing this invitation on me without forewarning means I'll have to attend. Not to do so would be betraying my best friend. To think I almost lost her this year. I swallow that unpleasant thought away, give myself a shake and turn back to the invitation.

You are invited to a fun weekend to celebrate
Amy Barnes's thirty-fifth birthday and her recent inheritance
Venue: Thistle Cottage, Blackwood Lane, Bucks.
Date: Thursday 18–Sunday 21 April
Partners invited overnight on Saturday for The Birthday evening!

A link to a map indicates the location of the cottage, which strikes me as a bit unnecessary, given that we shared a hall of residence situated further along Blackwood Lane, backing onto the edge of the forest. Blackwood Forest. As if we could ever forget that name. An involuntary shudder catches me unawares, as it does whenever the forest comes to mind, and I'm relieved when I hear Theo's key in the door and the thud of his bag as he drops it on the hall floor and appears in the doorway.

'Hi,' he says as I move to greet him. 'I won't get too close; I worked up a bit of a sweat walking home.'

'I can tell.' I sit back down, wrinkling my nose in exaggeration to hide my disappointment. It's only a small thing, but he always used to kiss me when he came in. But that was before. *We'll make this work.* His face glows with a healthy sheen, one of the benefits of being able to train outdoors. He's wearing Nike pants and sweatshirt, his sweaty kit left in his gym bag ready for the wash.

Theo is the most fastidious man I have ever met, and I'd bet he's the cleanest personal trainer around. Another good reason for us to stay together. I can't get out of the habit of listing the pros and cons of our relationship since the week we spent apart to decide our future. For me, the pros outnumber the cons. For him, I'm still not convinced, despite his assurances.

'Good day?'

'Yeah, it was, actually. Two new clients, both referrals from other clients. One wants twice-weekly meetings, the other has booked a trial session, so happy days. How about you?'

'Nothing out of the ordinary. Did a bit of lesson planning after school, then went straight to netball.'

'How many goals this time?'

'Three, but it was only a practice game. Our next proper match isn't for a while.' I close the laptop and stretch out my arms. 'I've put a lasagne in the oven.'

'Great, I'm starving. I'll just have a quick shower.'

'OK. Oh, and I've heard from Amy, she's finally organised her birthday do. I'll tell you over dinner.'

I prepare a salad and serve up the lasagne along with two glasses of sparkling water. Theo is the first partner I've had who doesn't drink, and since our decision to start a family, it's having a good effect on me. I can't remember the last time I opened a bottle of wine at home. The boiler whooshes as he showers, and I think about the invitation. I try to convince myself it would be good to get the old gang together again, and the party with all our partners should be fun, but no matter how positive a spin I try to put on it, I'm nervous. On the plus side, Theo has never been to Blackwood Forest before, and there are some great runs for him to do, trails already established by the many runners who use the wood. We could even stay an extra day, just the two of us, away from London and our busy lives. Maybe in a different part of Buckinghamshire, though, as the mere mention of Blackwood Forest makes my skin tingle.

Theo smells of apple shampoo when he reappears. His towel-dried hair looks darker blonde when it's damp, and he's shaved his stubble off, which makes him appear younger.

'Smells good,' he says as the aroma of baked cheese wafts around the kitchen. 'Anything I can do?'

'Just eat.'

We sit opposite one another on bar stools at the kitchen counter, which extends into the open-plan living room. Does it bother him too that we no longer hug when he comes home? In the old days that hug would often develop into a lingering kiss. A peck on the cheek would be a good start. *Give it time*, I tell myself; *we're getting on so much better than we were this time last month.*

I tell him about the birthday weekend while we eat.

'It falls in the Easter holidays, so that's not a problem. This term has felt like the longest ever.' I love teaching Year 6, but by the end of every term I'm ready to drop.

'So this is the cottage her aunt left her?'

'That's right.'

'Where is it?'

'It's in Blackwood, not far from where we went to university.'

Amy was the only student I knew who actually came from the area. At eighteen, most of us couldn't wait to get as far away from home as possible. Me and my sister would have ended up killing one another if I hadn't. I could never have foreseen how we'd all leave Blackwood as soon as our finals were over, returning briefly for graduation before scurrying back to our respective homes. Once again, Amy was the only one of us who stayed in the area. It must have been tough for her, an impossible choice, but her mother needed her.

'Will she move into the cottage?'

'I doubt it. She only bought her flat about two years ago. This has come out of the blue. Last time we spoke, she was still in shock about it. She'd been close to her aunt when she was younger, but they lost touch when the aunt had some kind of falling-out with Amy's mother, and this was totally unexpected. The aunt wasn't old, either. In any case, I can't imagine Amy would want to move in.'

'Why not?'

'The cottage is small, and it's on the edge of a huge forest. It's a bit creepy. I wouldn't want to live there.'

'It would be great for walking and running.'

'I knew you'd think that. And yes, it would, although …' I concentrate on a particularly chewy piece of lasagne, not wanting him to pick up on my discomfort. I didn't plan *not* to tell him what had happened back at university, but given that I preferred to shove the memories out of my mind whenever they made an unfortunate appearance, I'd just never got round to it.

He finishes his food and pushes his plate away.

'Although?'

'Nothing important. Did you enjoy that?'

'Great, thanks. Are you not going to finish yours?'

The half-eaten lasagne on my plate no longer looks appetising. I slide it towards him and he tucks in eagerly. Theo eats more than any other man I've been out with, on account of all the energy he uses up at work.

'So it's a long weekend for the women, with the men arriving for the main event? Sounds good to me.'

'Not just men. Kat's got a partner now.'

'Oh yes, I forgot, though from what you've told me, her relationships don't normally last that long. Who says they'll still be together by Easter?'

'Theo! That's only two weeks away.' He's right, though, of course. Kat's always been a bit of a free spirit, no matter how much she moans about wanting to settle down. 'Jade might well be the one. She's been around for a good few months now, and Kat sounded pretty smitten last time I spoke to her. Jade and I hit it off straight away, so I hope it works out.'

'Good for her.'

'You know what this means, though?' I look at him directly, struck as I always am by how much I love him, wishing I could be sure he felt the same way, hating the niggling doubt that won't quite go no matter how many times we've seen the relationship counsellor.

'No, what?' He gathers the plates together and takes them over to the sink, raising his voice as he turns the hot tap on full.

'Daisy.'

'Ah, yes. You haven't seen her since that evening, have you? How long ago is it now?'

'Six months. I've been meaning to ring her but kept putting it off. This invite is deliberate on Amy's part. The four of us were a really tight group at university and she wants us all back together like we used to be. I can understand why, given what a tough year she's had.'

'Give Daisy a ring. I'm sure she's been meaning to ring you too. And she'll have had her invitation, so it will no doubt be on her mind. I bet she'll be happy to hear from you.'

'When did you get so wise?' Our eyes meet and I look away, wishing my tongue didn't run away with me. We've spent the last nine months in counselling, and Theo has become very good at articulating his emotions in front of the therapist – too good at times.

'You're right,' I say. 'I'll give her a ring. We need to sort it out before the party, to make sure we're cool with each other before we get there. For Amy's sake, if nothing else.'

'I guess it's possible she won't go,' he says, plunging his hands into the sink, then quickly jumping backwards. 'Ouch. Jeez, that's hot.'

The suggestion floats through my mind, a lifeline. Daisy might say no and Kat will be busy; Amy will cancel and the weekend won't happen, we won't need to go back to Blackwood and confront the ghost that awaits us.

If only.

CHAPTER TWO

'Do you fancy watching another episode of that drama this evening?' Theo scrolls through the TV guide, legs stretched in front of him. He used to stretch them across my lap not so long ago. *Baby steps.*

'Can we save it for tomorrow? I'd rather phone Amy, talk about the birthday.'

'I'm out with work tomorrow night; it's Billy's leaving do. Drinks then a curry. You're welcome to join us if you like.'

'Yeah, I might.' Whenever Theo mentions work, flashing lights go off in my head. But he wouldn't have asked me before and I appreciate that he's making an effort. He's told me the woman he had an affair with has left the company, and I believe him. I have to.

I take my phone into the bedroom.

Amy picks up straight away. 'I knew you'd call,' she says. 'What do you think?'

'The party on the Saturday, is that just us lot, or are you inviting all your friends? Is it a proper party, that's what I mean.'

'No, just us. You haven't read the invitation correctly. Can you see the word *party*? It's more of a gathering, a select few of my old friends.'

'Are you sure? It's your thirty-fifth, Amy, and you've just been given the all-clear. I thought you'd be having a Kate Moss-style blowout lasting at least a week.'

'You've not been on social media lately, have you? You need to keep up. Kate's calmed down a lot in recent years, and so have

I. Everything feels different now. I still can't believe the past year isn't a dream.'

'I wish it was, Ames, you don't know how much.'

I was the first person Amy told about the lump she'd found – *smaller than a pea, most likely nothing* – and I was the one who accompanied her to the hospital when she was asked to come in to discuss the results of her tests, who held her hand and asked all the questions Amy was too shocked to ask. But work meant I couldn't be there every time she went for a round of chemotherapy, and her vast support network stepped in. Just over twelve months later, she is in remission and her life has changed. She stepped down from her post as head of English at a secondary school and now teaches part-time only, spending her spare time training to be a yoga teacher.

'I don't,' Amy says. 'My priorities have changed, and I know what's important.'

Hence the toned-down celebration. 'Are you sure? Never mind your birthday, you've got so much else to celebrate. There's nothing wrong with having a party.'

'I *am* sure,' she tells me. 'I want to be with my closest friends.'

'I know exactly what you're doing,' I say, curling into the armchair. 'It's not a party, it's a reunion.'

She doesn't respond.

'Are you sure this is a good idea?'

'Yes. I've given it a lot of thought. We need closure, and I've thought of a way of getting it.'

'How—'

'No questions, Lou, it's a surprise. You know you can trust me, right?'

'I guess.' My mind is whirring with possibilities of what she might be planning.

'I saw Kat had replied, but not Daisy. Has she rung you?'

'No, not yet.'

Silence lingers between us. I'm working out the best way to phrase what I want to say when Amy speaks.

'I know going back there is difficult, but it's really important to me, Lou. Inheriting this cottage feels like a sign. As if my aunt is trying to tell me something. We were close back then. She moved abroad around the time I finished uni.'

While Kat went travelling after graduation, and Daisy and I went home to our parents, wanting comfort food and parental pampering – we needed nurturing back to life – Amy never had anyone to look out for her, given her mother's poor health. It took her a while to work out what she wanted to do as a career, and teacher training made perfect sense. She had the gift of relating to people, and a strong desire to help and motivate others, to build communities. Hence the reunion.

'What about the location, Amy? Do you really want to go down that route? It's right on the edge of the forest.'

Blackwood Forest is a huge area of ancient woodland close to the university. In our first and final years, we thought we were lucky to be housed in halls of residence that bordered it. Undeniably beautiful, it's a favourite walking area for students and locals alike. On several occasions in our first year, we'd sit up all night talking, bleary-eyed and fuelled by cigarettes and tea, slipping out at dawn to walk through the hush of the early-morning forest, where woodpeckers tapped into the silence. I can't imagine ever wanting to do such a thing now. Staying up all night is one thing, but choosing to go into those woods … The thought gives me goosebumps.

It's sad how one experience can tarnish your view of the world. By the time I'd finished my final exam, the roots of the forest were creeping under my life and causing the earth to crack beneath my feet. I couldn't wait to leave the area.

'Of course I've thought about it. How could I forget its significance? But this is the perfect opportunity to exorcise our demons.

You know how I reacted when I found out about my aunt leaving me the cottage – my first inclination was not to go back at all, not even to check the place over, but to let the solicitor deal with the sale without involving me. I'm so glad I didn't. Now that I've been to see it, I feel differently. It's such a sweet place, you'll love it, I know you will.'

I'm not convinced. Amy has a far more optimistic nature than I do. Where she sees sweetness, I'm narrowing my eyes and noticing the cracks in the ceiling.

It's a big thing for us all to go back.

'I'm not planning on living there. I just thought I might as well make use of it.'

'Don't be surprised if the others aren't keen either,' I say. 'There's a reason we've all stayed away, chosen to live our lives as far away from Blackwood Forest as possible. Maybe you should have a plan B in case this doesn't work out.'

'There is no plan B.' Amy sounds determined. 'It's time to go back, I feel it in my gut. I need answers and I think you all do too. Don't let me down, Louise. We owe it to Hannah.'

CHAPTER THREE

The Thursday of Easter weekend soon arrives. I'm up at seven and showering before dressing in my new jeans, short-sleeved white shirt and heeled boots. My blonde hair is shoulder length and I'm pleased with my new haircut; it's the first time in years I've had a fringe and it makes me look younger. Before I leave, I double-check I've packed my folic acid – yes, it's safely in my handbag – then snap the bag shut with a satisfied click, enjoying the swoop of excitement that follows. It's finally happening – we're actually trying for a baby.

My case is in the boot and I settle into the rhythm of the motorway, tapping my foot along to the radio, relieved not to be travelling on Friday with all the other holidaymakers. An early start means I can spend some time with Amy before Kat and Daisy arrive.

I met Amy during my first week at university: a blur of parties and societies and drinks at bars with people I didn't know, all desperate to make a connection, to fill the hole left by those friends from school or college we'd been forced to leave behind. Each of us taking tentative steps towards adulthood. The week was a flurry of excitement and anxiety, culminating in a reception evening in the arts centre, where we could have a drink and meet other students.

I'd arrived ridiculously early, dressed carefully in my new jeans and leather jacket, aiming for the right image of relaxed and trendy, an interesting person to get to know, hoping the nerves bundled inside me were well hidden. One of the lecturers – scruffy suit and shiny bald head – ushered me in, leading me across to the only other person on her own in the room, who turned out to be Amy. Her artificially red hair was a mass of soft shoulder-length curls, and denim dungarees flattered her curvy figure. She was a local, she told me as she sorted me out with a drink, one of the rare breed of students who hadn't strayed too far from home. Her single mother was an academic – 'not here at Bucks, thank God, way too embarrassing' – and she loved the area, so why spend money travelling when there was a good university on her doorstep? She was living on campus for the first year in order to get the most out of university life. When I got to know her better, I learned her mother hadn't been able to work for months due to health issues, and relied on Amy for support. Bucks was the only university she had applied to. Conversation flowed between us, and by the time I'd finished my drink, the room had filled up around us and I felt as if I'd known her forever.

I turn my attention to the motorway and spend most of the journey overtaking vehicles in the slow lane. The car moves smoothly and I enjoy the feeling of control and independence that driving gives me, relieved that I don't have to suffer Theo's erratic driving style, holding my breath whenever he overtakes and arriving at our destination a bag of nerves. After his initial enthusiasm for the weekend, I sensed some reluctance, but he insisted it was all in my head, showing me his train booking for Saturday morning.

The satnav tells me to turn off at the next exit, and I slow down before deftly moving into the left-hand lane, the indicator clicking along with my thoughts. I wonder what the cottage will be like. When Amy received the letter from the solicitor, she was convinced it was some kind of joke, unaware that her aunt had owned any property in the area. She'd imagined a run-down shack in the middle of the forest, but the reality was apparently quite different – the solicitor had sent her some photographs – a picture-book cottage with a thatched roof and a bright yellow door. It had been well looked after, as her aunt had rented it to a friend for the last few years.

By the time I pull up at the cottage, it's late morning and I'm in need of a coffee. Amy must have heard the car crunching over the gravel, because she emerges from the front door, resplendent in a flowery jumpsuit, her red hair curling around her face, almost as long now as she used to wear it before the chemotherapy. Her face breaks into a wide smile and she hugs me to her. I feel bones that used to be covered and hold her tighter.

'How was the journey?'

'Great, thanks.' I fetch my case from the boot. 'The traffic wasn't too bad and it only took two hours.' I step back to study her. 'You look really well. I'm so pleased to see you.'

'Me too,' Amy says, putting her arm through mine. 'Shall I give you the tour?'

'Coffee first,' I say, and she laughs.

'Of course.'

'Although … I've brought along some decaf.' I feel my cheeks colour up, not ready to share my news just yet. 'I'm on a bit of a health kick at the moment.'

'Decaf's fine by me.'

The cottage is as pretty as she's told me, and the yellow door stands open. I sit at the large wooden table in the country-style kitchen as Amy pours water into a cafetière and puts it on the table between us. The smell of baking hangs in the air, and two fresh loaves sit on the side.

'What a delicious smell. You have been busy,' I say. 'It's a lovely place.' She's put her stamp on the cottage already: a glorious red teapot and a set of mugs painted with poppies brighten up the counter, and a huge vase of pink and white tulips sits on the table.

'Isn't it?'

Sun is pouring through the window, filling the kitchen with light. It's only small, but it feels homely. We both look out at the view of the back garden, and my eyes are drawn across the newly cut lawn, down the stepping-stoned path and beyond the small wooden shed, pulled as if by a magnet to the edge of the forest visible in the distance. A thick mass of tall trees lurks, the treetops huddled together, protecting the darkness contained between them. The sun slips behind a cloud and a dark shadow falls on the lawn, and I shiver as if I'm standing out there, experiencing the sudden drop in temperature.

Amy turns to face me.

'You're thinking about Hannah, aren't you?'

CHAPTER FOUR

I push the filter down hard onto the coffee grounds to avoid Amy's gaze. 'I can't help it,' I say. 'Mention Blackwood Forest and Hannah's face springs into my mind, and not Hannah as I remember her, but that wretched photo the newspapers plastered everywhere – she hated that one.'

I pour coffee into the two mugs Amy has placed between us, and add milk. I sip at my drink, needing warmth.

'But let's not talk about that just now. Tell me about the weekend. The others are coming, aren't they?' My voice sounds hopeful, but part of me still hopes for a cancellation, a last-minute reprieve.

'As far as I know. They should arrive later today, so I thought we could eat out this evening. I've got some activities planned for tomorrow. Lots of catching-up to do, chilling out, drinking …'

'Sounds good to me.'

'Have you talked to either of them since we last spoke?'

'Kat, yes, a few times. We've got a lot closer over the last few months. She's been so supportive over this stuff with Theo.'

Kat was there for me at one of the lowest points of my life. I'd accidentally found a note in Theo's jacket pocket, when I was looking for a lost key. If it had just been the note, I might not have taken it seriously, but I'd had my suspicions for months that he was seeing someone else. There were the usual clichés: late nights at the pub after work; a sprucing-up of his wardrobe; rolling over and claiming tiredness whenever I attempted a caress or a kiss. A hint of unfamiliar perfume in the air. So many nights I'd lain awake staring at his broad back, seeing it as a wall between us, when once we'd been so close. How had this happened?

The note led to a confession, almost as if he wanted to be found out. The words came spilling out and I could see he was mortified at what he'd done. I insisted he move back to his old flat for a while to let me mull things over, and it was during this period that I last saw Kat, when I had a monumental decision in front of me. I drove to her studio and chewed over my dilemma with her. Should I give him another chance? Or throw away five good years? At the age of thirty-five, could I face being single and childless? This was not how my life was meant to pan out. My dream of being a mother was floating away, and I felt washed up, a failure. It was this, and my belief in Theo's remorse at what he'd done, that helped me make my decision.

I felt better after pouring my heart out over a bottle of wine. I left my car and walked home reassured by Kat's words and the warm atmosphere of her studio, with weird sculptures dotted around the space and colourful abstract paintings on the walls. Kat lives in one of those uber-trendy live/work spaces in an old warehouse conversion. One half of the large open area is her art studio and the other is where she eats and sleeps. Despite her life being a whirlwind of social activity full of fellow creatives, she made time for me, and it meant a lot.

'She really helped me,' I add.

'What about Daisy?'

'No. I've been meaning to ring her but ran out of time. It means we haven't had a chance to talk about that last time we met and put it to bed, which is what I wanted to do.'

'You'll have plenty of time before Saturday, if you want to have a chat before Sam and Theo arrive. I can't wait for us all to be together again.'

I nod, and we're silent for a moment, a silence that buzzes with undercurrents, both of us knowing we can never all be together again in the same way, wondering how it will work out. I'd been holding onto the hope that Sam might not make it, but of course he was going to accompany his wife. As always, I feel a pang of guilt about the knowledge that only Daisy and I share: the burden I've lived with all this time, which makes it even harder for me to be in Sam's company. And it's not the only secret I'm keeping from Amy.

'You must have realised it might be difficult,' I say. 'But that's why you've done this, isn't it?'

She nods. 'It's time we sorted this out.' She pours us both more coffee. 'How's Theo?'

'He's good, we're good.' The words don't carry the conviction they should.

'Are you sure?' Amy raises her right eyebrow, a look I know well. Usually it means she's seen straight through me.

'Yes, I am sure. It's just me making problems where there aren't any. We had nine months with a marriage counsellor, who said from the beginning that she could see we both wanted to make it work. I told Theo everything I wanted to say, and I think he did too, and we came to the conclusion that we both wanted the same thing, which was a fresh start, possibly even a geographical move.' I don't want to tell her Theo has finally agreed to try for a family, in case I jinx it.

'That's great. I'm so happy for you. You are good together, you know; I've always thought you were well suited, and I really like him. But you don't sound convinced.'

'Like I said, it's just me. Despite thrashing everything out with him about the affair and letting him know exactly how I felt about it, I can't help having the occasional doubt. For example, if he says he's been out for a drink, I immediately wonder if he's telling me the truth. I have to give myself a stern talking-to, reprogramme the way I think. Basically I have to trust him, otherwise it's over before we've even started. He doesn't work with her any more, that's something at least. But I've made a choice and I'm sticking to it.'

'Does he know you still have doubts?'

'No way, that would be the end. We agreed to draw a line under it and concentrate on the future. He has to believe I trust him.'

'Don't beat yourself up so much. It's a very hard thing to do. I'm sure it will be the same for him, dealing with guilt. If the doubts continue, talking always helps.' She clears her throat. 'That ties in with why I've invited you all here. We need to clear the air. Imagine if the past wasn't hanging over us any longer. Wouldn't that be liberating?'

'In theory, yes, but … it's been such a long time.' My throat feels dry, but it's going to happen, there's no going back now. 'You're right. We might as well try.'

Amy smiles at me as if I've passed a test, then jumps to her feet, the tension evaporating. Sunlight floods the kitchen again as the cloud finally shifts.

'Come on, let me show you around. There are two bedrooms – you're in with me, if that's OK, then on Saturday we'll do a bit of shuffling around to fit everyone in.'

The bedrooms are small, with flowery wallpaper and old-fashioned furniture. I'd have preferred a room at the front of the house, instead of the view over the back garden. I park my case under the window and look out at the daffodils that cover the lawn in a zigzag pattern. The yellow flowers stand out against the dark mass of the forest in the background, and I focus on them, willing their light to block out the memory of the way I used to feel standing in the forest surrounded by the tall trees with their deep green foliage. I shift my gaze back to the room.

'What time are the others arriving?'

'Not until late afternoon. We can have some lunch and then go for a walk if you like; might as well make the most of the weather. It looks like it's going to be glorious for Easter.'

*

After a lunch of a leek and courgette tart, baked by Amy the day before, accompanied by a selection of salads, we set off for a walk. The river path is busy with other walkers, and a fair few cyclists and runners go past, meaning we walk in single file most of the way, lost in our own thoughts, enjoying the ease of each other's company that comes with a long friendship. After about twenty minutes, I flop down on a bench.

'You look tired,' Amy says, her eyebrows meeting in concern.

'I didn't sleep well last night.' Or any night since I received the invitation. Night-time is when the worries I've managed to stamp out during the day scurry back into my head like beetles, the reality of us all being together again playing out in my mind.

'You *are* worrying about Theo.'

'No, it's not that. Do you really need me to spell it out?'

Amy shifts position on the bench, putting distance between us.

'It's Sam, isn't it?'

'Of course it's Sam. The four of us meeting up again is going to be emotional enough, but Sam … you know how I feel about him.'

Sam. Sam and Hannah. Hannah and Sam. Hannah and I met him at the same time. Six foot of handsomeness. Friendly, open face. He captained the university cricket team, and was a popular, easy-going guy with a gentle side to him. They were so right for one another that none of us ever questioned it, until Sam did the unthinkable and went off with Daisy.

It's always hard when couples split and you have to make a choice about whose side to take, but even though they both became my friends, Hannah was my closest friend at uni. Amy and I only became close afterwards, when events pushed us together; when Sam delivered the bombshell that blew our close-knit group apart. He had driven Hannah to a desperate place and none of us were able to pull her back, and for that I could never forgive him. When you've seen a heartbroken woman, it cuts deep, and Hannah's heart had been shredded to pieces. I'd made an effort with Sam, I really had, for Daisy's sake, but it wasn't easy, and being back here in Blackwood had brought it all to the fore again.

'But you went out for that dinner with him. I thought you'd be OK with it.'

'And look how that went. Besides, Theo was there, and he doesn't know about any of that. Or about Hannah.'

'Why haven't you told him?'

'Because what happened to Hannah is like having a shadow behind everything I do in my life, and I want me and Theo to be free of that. You feel it too, don't you?'

Amy nods. 'But Sam won't be here for the whole weekend. Talking to Daisy will help, I'm sure. Honestly, it won't be as bad as you expect. It's my birthday, and I'm determined we're all going to have fun. Come on, let's get back now.'

We reach the steps leading away from the river and move into single file again, pausing for a moment to catch our breath at the top of the steps before setting off along the lane. The forest is in view now, dark like a threatening thundercloud suspended in the sky.

'I do understand,' Amy says as we approach the cottage, 'which is why this weekend is so important.'

A breeze lifts my hair as Amy unlocks the yellow door and steps inside. I hesitate on the doorstep, reluctant to go in, but it's too late now: I'm here, and the weekend is in motion. A feeling of unease makes the skin at the back of my neck prickle as I follow her into the cottage. The forest pulls like a magnet, and I turn back to look at it again: the place where fourteen years ago, Hannah followed the path through the trees and never came back out. I hope we are doing the right thing.

Blackwood Independent, 26 April 2005

A student from Buckinghamshire University has gone missing.

Hannah Robinson, 21, was last seen on Monday 25 April after a lecture in the arts building on the university campus. The building is situated on Bertram Lane, on the eastern side of the campus, a mile away from Blackwood Forest. She was seen leaving the lecture theatre at just after five o'clock.

Close friends say it is out of character for her to disappear for such a long period of time without keeping in touch.

Hannah is five foot nine and of slim build, with waist-length fair hair. Anyone with information is asked to contact Blackwood police station.

CHAPTER FIVE

Amy pours us a couple of glasses of water and we sit out in the back garden, a decent-sized space with a small table on the flagstones outside the back door. The forest is out of sight when we're seated, but the trickle of fear I felt just now hasn't left me.

'Just being in Blackwood where it happened brings it all back, doesn't it? I can't look at that bloody forest without remembering Hannah, and it's going to be the same for all of us. You said you want to talk about the past, but why now, specifically? Has something happened?'

Amy sighs. 'You always see through me.'

'Yes, I do. You don't do anything without careful planning, and I want to know what's up. I won't say anything to the others.'

'Of course I want to discuss it; I didn't want to jump into it the minute you arrived, that's all. We've got so much else to catch up on.'

'And we've got the whole weekend. We might as well make use of the time before the others arrive.'

'OK, well, this may not be news to you, but have you heard anything about a podcast?'

'No, about what?' Unease flickers inside me.

'What do you think? About Hannah. This guy got in touch with my mother. He's a former journalist, fairly well known around here, and he's setting up a new podcast about people who have gone missing in the county. Hannah's story is one he's going to feature. He asked my mother for my contact details. Mum was a bit of a guard dog during my illness; she acted like a gatekeeper, not wanting anyone or anything to upset me. He got in touch when I was still having chemo, and she told him I was unwell and she'd pass his details on. Said I'd get in touch later if I was interested.'

'What's his angle?'

'Mental health. Mum said he sounded genuinely concerned about a spate of suicides amongst young people in Buckinghamshire, spanning several years.'

'Are you going to talk to him?'

'I haven't decided. I wanted to speak to you guys first. I still can't believe Hannah would kill herself.'

'Don't beat yourself up about it. I'm exactly the same. She could have reached out to any of us, but she chose not to, and that's what hurts. We have to accept it and move on.'

Amy doesn't look convinced. 'Mum said the guy asked her if we'd ever thought they'd got it wrong.' Her look is direct, her eyes sorrowful.

'You mean the suicide verdict?'

She nods, just as a shrill ring bursts through the air, making me jump. Water spills from my glass, a cold splat on my leg. My hand feels unsteady as I wipe it away.

'It's Kat,' Amy says as she reads the message.

Questions are bubbling on my tongue.

'Do *you* think they got it wrong? That her death was an accident?'

Amy doesn't answer.

'Surely you don't think … someone else was involved? Not suicide, but—'

'I don't know.' She looks back at her phone. 'I don't want to go into it now. Kat's on her way; she managed to get off work early. I assume Jade will be joining us on Saturday. I'm so pleased she's finally met someone.'

'Jade is great for her. It's your turn next.'

'Do you know what – I think I'm ready to date again.'

'Yes. High five.' We slap hands, although my gesture lacks energy – I'm still reeling from what Amy has just said.

Amy is blushing. 'It's not such a big deal.'

'Of course it is. Amy Barnes is back in town. It means you've reached an important milestone – and that you're finally over Phil.'

'He did me a favour by walking out. What I had with him wasn't love, I can see that with hindsight. I'm much clearer now about what I want from the people in my life. It's the start of a whole new chapter.'

She sits back in her chair and a smile spreads across her face. I'd like to probe her further on what she meant about Hannah, but now is not the time.

'It feels good, actually, because I never thought I'd get to this point. After Phil left—'

'That coward. I'll never forgive him for that.'

Philip and Amy had just celebrated three years together the week she was diagnosed with breast cancer. Within a week, he'd moved out. He went to work one morning and didn't come home. Amy was in bits. So I can understand why she's wary.

'When I was at my lowest, probably the point at which I shaved my hair off, I remember looking in the mirror and thinking nobody would ever want me again. Last week I looked in the mirror and do you know what? I said to myself, "You've still got it, girl." Then I went straight out and bought this jumpsuit.'

'It's lovely.'

'Thanks. I deserve to have someone special to share my life with and to snuggle up to and lean on when the going gets tough. This time I'll make sure I choose more carefully.'

'Which is where I come in.'

'Which is where you come in. My thoughts exactly. You're a good judge of character and you're a whizz with apps. Online dating. Where do I start?'

'Luckily for you, one of my colleagues never stops talking about her dates, so I know quite a lot about it. She's told me the sites she likes best. We can have a look through them together. I'm sure the others will want to help. You can show us what kind of look you're going for.'

'Look? I'll make sure I go way beyond that this time. Phil was drop-dead gorgeous, but under the surface he was pretty selfish. It just took me a while to notice. I should have realised when he made me stop going to my evening class. He hated me going out without him.'

'I wanted to say something at the time, but you were infatuated.'

'Don't. Being infatuated is not a state I plan to get into again. You'd have thought I'd learned my lesson with Joe – I was so preoccupied with him when Hannah disappeared, and I've never forgiven myself.'

We sit in silence for a moment, both of us grappling with the guilt that never goes away.

'Let's be positive. I'll help you find someone online. Make a list of what attributes you want.'

'Yeah, great idea. You can screen them all for me.'

'Think of me as your agent.'

We pick up our glasses and take them indoors. It will be hard to keep my mind on Amy's love life now that she's dropped the doubt about Hannah like a grenade into my lap and run off before it detonates. If she doesn't think it was an accident … My mind wants to leap to all kinds of conclusions. At least she's given me time to think about it before the others arrive, when I've no doubt we'll discuss it together.

Half an hour later, I've unpacked my case in the small room I'm sharing with Amy. Two single beds just about fit into it. The bed by the window has a small moth-eaten teddy bear on it that I recognise from university days. Mr Ted. Pain grips my chest and I reach for the wall to steady myself from the unexpected shock. He used to sit on Hannah's bed, and I'm transported back to her campus room, the university-issue duvet cover with brown swirls, Mr Ted on the pillow. 'Look what Sam gave me,' she said, a sparkle in her eyes. That was the moment I knew they were serious. I'm surprised to see him here.

Amy appears in the doorway.

'You remember him?'

'Of course. I didn't know you had him.'

She sits on her bed. 'I helped her parents pack up the room. They couldn't face it. Her mum asked if I wanted anything.' She picks up the teddy and holds him to her face, inhales his scent. 'I like to think he smells of her.' Her eyes are full of tears; my arms go around her and we hold each other tight.

'We need to feed you up a bit,' I say to lighten the mood, not wanting to dwell on the past.

'I'm trying,' she says, wiping her eyes with the back of her hand. 'Some days I still get really tired. I usually have a little nap around now. You can amuse yourself for half an hour, can't you? Keep an ear out for Kat.'

'Of course. I'll take my book out into the garden. See you in a bit.'

On my way downstairs, I glance out of the window from the upstairs landing, my attention caught by a black Mini Cooper pulling up in front of the house. So much for reading that book. Kat emerges looking as chic as her car, dressed in an oversized black jacket, dark skinny trousers with strategically placed zips, and chunky boots. Seeing her always makes me wish I'd made more of an effort than my usual shirt and jeans. She smooths down her clothes and extracts a smart leather holdall from the back seat of the car.

I'm about to go down to let her in when she takes a packet of cigarettes from the bag, lights one up and walks away from the cottage along the lane. That's unexpected. Kat gave up smoking ages ago. She disappears from view and I continue to watch from the landing. After about five minutes, she reappears, talking on her phone. She frowns as she presses the phone to her ear, stopping outside the cottage to take a look at the forest. I wave at her, and she looks up, eyes partly covered by her heavy fringe, then waves back. Her sleek brown bob swings as she walks up the path, and I run downstairs and out of the front door.

She swings her large leather bag over her shoulder.

'Kat.' I pull her to me and inhale tobacco and shampoo. We stand and look at the cottage.

'Cute place, isn't it?' she says. 'I'd forgotten what the roads are like round here. Talk about hidden.'

'None of us were driving back then, either.'

'True.' As if drawn by an invisible force, we both turn and look towards the forest.

'Never thought I'd come back here voluntarily,' she says, her voice quiet.

'Me neither. You'd better prepare yourself – Amy wants to talk to us about Hannah.'

Kat's expression darkens. 'That's what I was afraid of. Why now?'

I tell her about the podcast. 'And she's had a lot of time to think over the past year. She's acting as if she's got something to tell us.' Maybe I'm not the only one with secrets.

'Ah. The conversation we've all managed to avoid.' Her eyes dart to her car. 'Shall we leave now?'

We both grin, and the ice is broken.

'Come on,' I say. 'Once you get inside, you'll forget about where we are.' I'm trying to convince myself at the same time.

'Is Daisy here yet?'

I shake my head. 'She'll be here later. Did you ring her?'

'I did. Has she told you?'

'Told me what?'

'That Sam isn't coming. She said he had too much work on.'

'That means Theo will be the only man. Not that he'll mind, but …' My body relaxes – it will be so much easier without Sam.

'Where is Amy anyway?'

'Having a nap.'

'Worn her out already with your witty repartee, have you?'

'Ha ha. Come inside and I'll make some coffee.'

Kat goes to the bathroom while I sort out the drinks. The kettle is an old-fashioned one that requires heating on the stove. It's fiddly and hard to light, and I'm not paying attention. My mind is on the doubt Amy sowed earlier; I wonder too how Sam's non-attendance will affect the weekend. The flame whips up the matchstick and licks my fingers, and I blow hard on the burn, cursing. Cold water soothes my skin but not my doubts. What if Amy was right about Hannah? What if this weekend she plans to blow everything apart?

CHAPTER SIX

Kat was the first to contact me after Amy sent the invitation. Her email arrived the same evening.

Hey Lou,

How's it going? Got your invite?! It's not exactly the wild party I was expecting, but I guess her 21st set the bar high, and we are getting on a bit now, aren't we?!! Jade was 30 last week and you'd think she'd just reached pensionable age the way she's been going on about it! I plan to celebrate my 35th with an all-nighter and an outrageous tattoo – just need to decide on which part of my body!

You and Theo will be there, won't you – need to be sure before I commit. I haven't been back to Blackwood since I left university and my parents relocated to Cornwall. Not sure how I feel about it. I'm surprised she chose to hold the party there, but that's Amy for you, always full of surprises. Lucky her, too – I wish someone would leave me a house! Shall I organise a present, from the three of us? I'll ask Daisy too. Am happy to choose something. I presume Sam is going. Hope you've patched things up after your disagreement. Can't wait to see you all,

Kat x

PS Does Theo know about Hannah? I've never mentioned it to Jade.

The PS didn't fool me – tacked on as an apparent afterthought, but in reality the most important part of the email. Kat had read the invitation as I had, seen the birthday weekend as Amy's attempt to come to terms with the past, and wondered how this might play out with partners in tow, especially Sam.

I replied immediately.

Hi Kat,

Hello! Yes, I was surprised by the invitation, but Amy's had such a monumental year I guess we owe it to her to go along with her wishes. She's been angling to get us all together for ages. I suppose it had to happen one day. It might even do us all good.

Thanks for offering to sort out a present – that would be a big help. You know I'm rubbish at presents and you have such impeccable taste. Let me know how much you spend and I'll settle up with you. I'll bring some champagne. It will be nice for us girls to have a couple of days together before the others arrive. I'm sure we can keep Daisy in check!

Love,
Lou

'That's better.' Kat comes into the kitchen. 'It's so good to see you.'

She pulls me in for another hug, and I feel the hard muscles under her jacket. She works out at least once a day, has done for as long as I've known her. Another reason the smoking is out of character.

'You too.'

'Amy's upstairs, I presume?'

'Yes, she's in her room – our room, I should say. I'm in with her until Saturday. When Theo arrives, she'll sleep down here.'

'You mean …' Kat cocks her head, and I grin.

'Yep, you're in with Daisy.'

'Oh well, I guess I'll just have to try and keep tidy. I've got the present, by the way. I chose a silk scarf, but I had it gift-wrapped, so you won't be able to see it until we give it to her.'

'Great, thanks. How much do I owe you?'

She waves her hand in a dismissive gesture. 'Don't worry about it. How long have you been here?'

I give her the lowdown as I make the coffee. She wanders out into the garden, then has a quick nose around the ground floor.

'Nice place,' she says. 'Has she decided to keep it after all? It would make a great Airbnb. It's right on the doorstep of the forest.' We exchange a glance. 'That's a good thing, Lou, to most people. And we had some fun times here, once upon a time.' She looks wistful. 'Let's make sure Amy has a fabulous weekend.'

She changes the subject. 'How's Theo? You two are OK now, right?'

'Yes, I think so. We're talking about buying a place outside London, probably in Wales, where his family live.' I pour coffee into mugs and we sit down at the kitchen table.

'Cool,' Kat says. 'For you, that is. I can't imagine not living in the city.'

'You wouldn't last a week.' Kat hangs out in hipster cafés, eats out most nights, and goes clubbing at weekends. I wish I had her stamina. Clubbing no longer appeals to me, which helped when Theo and I were deciding our future. A big garden and pretty surroundings are more important to me now than the city buzz.

'What about Jade, how's it going?'

Kat pulls her mug towards her and blows on the hot liquid. 'She's OK.'

'Is she coming on Saturday?'

'I'm not sure.'

'It will be nice to see her,' I say, trying to read the slightly embarrassed look on Kat's face.

Footsteps sound in the hall and we both look round.

'Amy,' Kat says, jumping to her feet as Amy appears in the doorway. She gives her a hug. 'It's so good to see you. You look great.'

Amy joins us at the table and pours herself some coffee.

'How's work going?' she asks.

Kat nods. 'I'm doing OK. I've got an exhibition coming up in a couple of months' time.'

'Fabulous. In London?'

'Yes. You should come. You can stay with me. If you don't mind sleeping in my studio surrounded by spooky sculptures.'

'I'd love that. It's great that you're able to make a living doing what you love. That's what I'm hoping to do with my yoga eventually, teach it as a career.'

'I've proved my dad wrong, anyway. He said very few sculptors make it. I owe him, actually, not for much else, but that one sentence of his made me determined to succeed.'

'Same with Daisy: her family didn't want her to be an actress.'

I laugh. 'I can't imagine Daisy being anything else.'

'What time is she coming?' Kat asks. 'Have you heard from her?'

Amy nods. 'I just had a text. She'll be here in about an hour.'

'Great. You're sharing with her; I hope that's OK?'

'You owe me.' Kat grins. 'Lou's already briefed me. I'll be on my best behaviour.' She winks at me. 'I don't want a telling-off for leaving my clothes strewn around. This is a great cottage, Amy, and congratulations on the inheritance. You must be thrilled. Are you planning to rent it out?'

'I haven't decided yet. I've had so much time to think over the last few months, and one of the conclusions I came to was that I'm too old to be afraid. When you're faced with a threat to your health, your priorities change. Burying problems and running away from them doesn't work. I can't let the past rule my present. If I could make my peace with what happened, it might be good to move here; it would be nice and tranquil for my yoga. I'm sure it would help you guys too, to face those fears head on.'

We all lose ourselves in our thoughts for a moment.

'That was what was in my mind when I was wondering what to do to mark my birthday,' Amy eventually says. 'Thoughts I've had, things I've never said. I'm sure we must all feel like that about Hannah's disappearance.'

I'm not so sure, but I don't want to dampen her bubble. Some things are best kept secret. It's funny how we persist on calling it a disappearance. So much easier to face than the truth.

Kat's nodding, but I can't read her face.

'We owe it to Hannah,' Amy continues. 'Coming back here means facing up to each other, making peace with the area. It's a beautiful part of the world and we all have our roots here. That's why this weekend means so much to me.'

'I get it,' Kat says, 'but don't be surprised if it all goes pear-shaped.'

Do they both feel the creeping dread that slithers through me every time I recall the moment the truth about Hannah was revealed? Do they replay that moment over and over as I do, despite my attempts to suppress it? I've got better at shutting the thoughts out, but my unconscious will never let me forget, and the forest dream comes to me regularly. Despite Amy having voiced her intentions for the weekend, I can't bring myself to reveal my feelings to the others, because that would mean owning up to withholding details from the police. Instead the scene flashes before me, that defining moment in my life.

I was in my room on campus when I heard, supposedly writing an essay but unable to focus, flickers of worry running through my mind. I was going over my last conversations with Hannah, wondering what thoughts were inside her head and whether I should have pressed her to tell me why she was walking around with shoulders bent as if she was carrying a heavy load, willing her to get in touch, berating myself for not being more persistent when she insisted there was nothing wrong. She'd been missing for five days at that point and I was desperate to do something constructive. Writing an essay on medieval literature seemed futile. A loud knock at the door interrupted my thoughts. The warden of our hall of residence stood in the narrow corridor outside my room.

'Sorry to disturb you, Louise, but it's important. Could I have a word, please.'

As soon as I caught sight of the sympathetic look on his face, I knew. I could read that expression, and I understood in that moment that the worst had happened and I would never be able to speak to my friend again.

A flicker of fear rises in me at the thought of confronting these long-buried feelings. Does Amy know what she is doing, what emotions and behaviour she might be unleashing amongst our group? What if the others are holding on to secrets too?

Amy's voice interrupts my thoughts.

'Theo and Jade will be here to balance us out, be the voice of reason.'

Kat and I exchange glances.

'If Jade is even coming ...'

'She is, isn't she?' Amy asks. 'I was looking forward to seeing her.'

'I hope so,' Kat says. 'Can I finish this coffee?'

Face closed, shoulders stiff, she pours the remaining coffee from the cafetière. I recall the cigarette she smoked outside, the hungry way she sucked at it.

'I spotted you having a sneaky cigarette earlier,' I say. 'I didn't know you'd taken up smoking again. How come?'

She gives me a quizzical look. 'Are you spying on me?'

I laugh; I wasn't expecting her to sound so serious about it. 'I saw you from upstairs, when you arrived.'

She shrugs. 'I have one when I feel like it, more of a social thing. And you know me – I don't like rules.'

I can't see what was social about the cigarette she had earlier, but something about her tone warns me not to pursue the matter. I switch subjects. 'What's Daisy doing with the children?'

'Apparently her parents are having them for the weekend,' Amy says.

'What's wrong with Sam, the lazy bugger?' Kat folds her arms. 'Why can't he look after them?'

'I gather he's got some important work to finish off.' Amy looks at her. 'Have you seen them recently?'

'I haven't seen Sam since university, but I spoke to Daisy after I got your invitation. She was having problems settling Teddy into school, so that took up most of the conversation. She said she was looking forward to getting away from work and family for a bit.'

Amy's mobile vibrates and plays the sound of an old-fashioned phone ring.

'It's Daisy,' she says, and answers the call. I take my cup and deposit it in the sink. 'She's almost here. Let's go and meet her.'

A cab turns into the road as we step outside. Daisy jumps out and waits for the driver to remove her suitcase from the boot. Her long blonde hair is pulled into a loose knot and her sunglasses are propped on her head. She looks relaxed in jeans and a pastel lemon jacket, her face and nails immaculate.

I remember the first time I saw her on campus. I didn't know her then, but she had a presence, stood out with her unique personal style. Heads turned when she walked by, and she glowed with the knowledge.

She flashes a radiant smile at us.

'Thank you so much,' she tells the driver.

'I don't suppose …?'

'A photo?'

Kat grins and raises her eyebrows at me.

'Would you? It's for my wife. She was gutted when your character left *Appleside*.'

'Of course,' Daisy says, posing with the driver as he holds his phone aloft.

'Any chance you'll be coming back?'

'I couldn't possibly say.' She smiles mischievously. 'But the door was left open, so never say never.'

The driver waves out of the window as he pulls away.

'She's still got it,' Kat says.

Daisy wheels her case over. 'It's nice to be appreciated,' she says. Playing Jessie in the nation's favourite soap was her breakout role, and although she stopped work for a while to raise her family, I'm sure she'll be back on our screens again soon.

'It's lovely to see you all,' she says, her pretty face lighting up. 'What fun this weekend is going to be.'

CHAPTER SEVEN

'This is fabulous,' Daisy says in her melodic voice, looking around the pizzeria. There are only six tables, all empty bar one: six women wearing sparkly dresses, one of them sporting a tiara. A hen party; just our luck.

'Isn't it?' Amy says. 'I found it by chance. I'll cook a meal at the cottage tomorrow, but I wanted you to see this place.'

The chef pounds dough in the open kitchen at the back of the restaurant, twisting it with his hands and slapping it back down before kneading it again, arms working vigorously. The opportunity for me to speak to Daisy alone hasn't arisen yet, but she hasn't been unfriendly to me, so maybe she's over our last meeting. The group of women in the corner erupts with laughter. A waiter approaches with some menus.

'Let's order straight away,' Daisy says, before the rest of us have time to protest. 'I haven't eaten since lunchtime, which was hours ago.'

I scan the menu and make my choice, and the others follow suit. Once the pizzas are ordered, we choose a bottle of red and one of white, and an apple juice for me. I'm sitting next to Amy and opposite Kat.

'Have you got any work lined up?' Amy asks Daisy.

'I'm reading a couple of scripts my agent sent me, both television dramas. Now that the boys are in school, it's a lot easier.'

Daisy threw herself into her career after the loss of her first baby, and worked steadily, becoming one of those actresses people recognised, especially once she landed the role of Jessie in *Appleside*. It was several years before she got pregnant again, and now she has two boys. Motherhood suits her, and her face lights up when she talks about her children. Has she really forgotten?

'It's a shame Sam can't come on Saturday,' Amy says.

I nod in agreement, looking sympathetic, as if I share her sentiments.

'He is coming,' Daisy says. 'I put my foot down. It's ages since we've had any time away from the kids together, and it will do us good.'

I grab my glass of water to hide my confusion. I'd just got used to the idea of him not coming.

'That's great news,' Amy says. 'How is he doing? Apart from working too hard.'

'He's good. His business is doing well. He's just finished working on Stacey Greene's house in Hampstead.'

Amy looks blank. 'Presumably we should know who Stacey Greene is?'

Daisy rolls her eyes. 'She's a fashion designer. I thought everyone knew that.'

'Not me,' Amy says. 'But then I hardly ever watch TV. Except for when you're on, of course.'

'If you need your cottage redesigned, Amy, Sam will give you a good price.'

'I don't know what I'm doing with it yet,' she says.

I doubt any of us could afford Sam's rates; he has worked hard to build up his interior design business, and Daisy sends some good contacts his way. Unlike the rest of us, she never had to worry about getting a job in the supermarket in the evenings to supplement her income while she was at uni, but she never rubbed our noses in it and was always generous.

I unwrap a packet of breadsticks and nibble at the end of one. Last time I saw Sam was over a year ago when he left the restaurant with Daisy, one hand on her back, claiming he'd had an urgent call from the babysitter, all of us knowing it was a lie and that they just wanted to get away from me. He turned back to look at me before slipping through the door, and the expression on his face gives me goosebumps whenever I recall it. Like now.

'Louise.' Daisy's voice is loud. 'How many more times? Do you want red or white?'

'None for me, thanks.'

'Were you thinking about Theo?' Daisy asks, as she pours red for Kat, white for herself and Amy. As I always do, I wonder what's behind her question. These are my oldest friends and I shouldn't feel so tense. A glass of wine would relax me. Instead, I top up my water.

'I was thinking about my pizza, actually,' I say, and Kat laughs. 'Trust you.'

'Sam got on very well with Theo,' Daisy says. 'It's a shame we haven't seen more of him.'

'Well he'll be here on Saturday,' I say. 'He's looking forward to it. He's not been to this part of the world before.' *Luckily for him.*

Could I risk just one glass of wine? The bottle they've chosen is expensive, a step up from the supermarket specials I was drinking the week Theo and I spent apart. With his good influence out of the way, I was straight back to my old ways, using alcohol to drown my misery at his absence, and the images of him and his other woman I couldn't eradicate from my mind. *No.* I won't go back there.

The pizzas arrive and we tuck in; the waiter refreshes our glasses and we catch up with each other's news. Once our plates have been cleared and most of the wine has been drunk, we order coffee.

'Tell us about you and Theo,' Kat says. 'I gather you've come to a decision.' She gives me a knowing look and I'm grateful for her discretion.

I sip at my coffee, feeling less uncomfortable. I bring Daisy up to date with what's been happening.

'We've put it behind us. It's taken a while – things came to a head and we spent some time apart. After that we both agreed to try again and talked about what we needed to do to get the relationship back on track. Relationship therapy was the most significant decision we came to; we went to see someone for a while and we've just finished the sessions. I think Theo really regrets what he's done.'

'Will you be able to trust him?' Kat asks. 'I don't think I could, not if it happened to me.'

'I have to, otherwise we might as well give up now. We've agreed to start again.'

'What about the other woman?' asks Amy. 'Are you sure it's over?'

I stare into the flame of the tea light that flickers in front of me, seeing the face of the woman I've conjured up in my mind, clutching my hands together, wishing the image would leave me.

'She isn't working directly with him any longer, which helps.'

'Am I right in thinking you don't know her?' Kat asks.

I nod.

'If it was me, I'd have to find out every detail about her. It would drive me insane, wondering all the time.'

'Some people want to do that, but it would have killed me. He swears I don't know her, and I don't want to. She was after him for ages – not that I'm excusing his behaviour,' I add, not missing the glance exchanged between Daisy and Kat. 'It takes two and all that, but we were going through a rough patch at the time. Theo's in a good place now, we both are, and we've put it behind us. And' – I sip my water – 'you might as well know. We're trying for a baby.' My cheeks flush.

'So that's why you're not drinking.' Daisy looks at the glass in my hand. 'I thought you were just being a party pooper.'

'Honestly, Daisy, you sure know how to put a damper on a girl,' Kat says. 'That's great news, Lou. Let's have a toast to you and Theo and the new baby-to-be.' She raises her glass.

'Steady – you're getting a bit ahead of yourself.' But I'm grateful to Kat, and I glow with excitement, believing in this moment that it will happen and everything will be all right. 'Let's toast Amy, too. To your good health, Amy, and to a fabulous birthday weekend.'

'Cheers,' says Kat, and we all clink glasses.

Kat's phone, which is lying on the table, rings and Jade's photo flashes on the screen. 'I'll take this outside,' she says, scraping her chair back.

'Tell Jade we'll see her Saturday,' Daisy calls after her. 'I'm dying to meet her. I do hope she turns up. It won't be much of a party otherwise.'

'Of course it will, even if it's just us.'

'It's not exactly going to be a party with so few of us,' Amy says. 'Think of it more as a soirée.'

'A soirée,' Daisy says, rolling her tongue around the word. 'I like the sound of that. Will there be canapés and champagne?'

I watch Kat as she paces up and down in the street outside, cigarette in her hand. She cuts a restless figure. She pushes the door hard as she comes back in, irritation on her face until she sees me watching her and composes herself.

'Bad news?' I ask as she sits down, the smell of tobacco lingering around her.

'No, everything's fine.'

'Jade is coming on Saturday, isn't she?' Daisy asks.

'I'm not sure, OK? Leave it, will you, Daisy.' Kat looks to see where the waiter is. 'Let's get the bill.'

Daisy looks disgruntled. 'I was only asking. I was looking forward to meeting her, that's all.'

The waiter appears and Kat takes the bill from him. 'I'll split it between us.'

Daisy raises an eyebrow over Kat's bent head, watching her calculate the totals on her phone, stabbing at the numbers with her finger. Once she's finished, she tells us what we each owe and drops her bank card on top of the bill.

'It's contactless. I'll wait for you outside,' she says, shrugging her leather jacket on. 'It's stuffy in here.'

CHAPTER EIGHT

Back at the cottage, Kat goes straight up to bed.

'What's up with her?' Daisy asks. 'Is it just me, or is she in a funny mood? I hope she's not going to be like it all weekend.' She wanders around the kitchen looking in cupboards, a habit she's had since university days – she always appears at ease wherever she is. 'I was rather looking forward to this weekend.'

'She's probably tired,' I say. 'She's not normally like that.'

'It sounds like she's having problems with Jade,' Amy says. 'Has she said anything to you?'

'No.' I can't imagine that's the case. I've talked to Kat about Theo a lot over the past few weeks. Surely she'd have said something if she was having problems herself? I recall the fleeting expression on her face when we spoke outside – maybe I'm not the only one feeling threatened by being here.

'Maybe she's just having a bad day.'

'Aha,' Daisy says, holding up a bottle of Baileys. 'Anyone fancy a nightcap?'

'Where on earth did you dig that up from?' Amy says. 'It must be years old.'

'No worries,' Daisy says, her voice loud, animated after a few drinks. 'Mature is good, and quite frankly, anything will hit the spot right now. I haven't had a girly night for ages. Who's going to join me?'

'Not me, I'm whacked,' Amy says.

'Louise?' A challenge glints in Daisy's eyes as she looks at me. The food and company have made me feel warm and mellow. I should take advantage of this chance to have a heart-to-heart with Daisy.

'I'll keep you company, but I'll stick to tea. I won't be too long, Amy, and I promise I'll be quiet when I come up.'

'As long as you're able to take part in tomorrow's activities, I don't care how long you stay up. I've got peppermint tea if you want that.'

'*Activities* sounds a bit formal,' Daisy says. 'Should I be worried?'

'No.' Amy laughs.

'I hope Grumpy is asleep when I go up. I don't want another tongue-lashing from her.'

'I'm sure you can give as good as you get,' I say.

'Play nice, ladies,' Amy says, taking a glass of water upstairs with her. 'See you in the morning.'

Daisy puts the bottle of Baileys on the table between us and pours herself a small measure in a wine glass.

'Perfect,' she says after the first sip, licking the cream from her lips. Her lipstick is as fresh as it was at the beginning of the evening, unlike mine, which is long gone. Next to Daisy, I always feel as if I've lost my shine. 'Sure I can't tempt you?'

'Go on then, just a taste.'

I take a small sip. It's not my favourite drink, but I don't want to antagonise Daisy, to spoil this opportunity to talk things over.

'I'm sorry to hear about you and Theo,' she says. 'I had no idea. It must have been awful.'

'Understatement. But thanks. And we're back on track now.'

'I was surprised to hear you want kids, though.'

'Oh. Why?'

'You're surrounded by them at work all day. I've always assumed you didn't want any of your own.'

'I love kids. Why do you think I chose to be a primary school teacher? I've always known I'd have a family one day, but it's not something I've talked about much. There didn't seem much point until I was in a position to make it happen. Which is now, hopefully.'

'But what if he does it again? Leopards, spots and all that.'

'I can't afford to think like that. I have to trust him.'

'I couldn't do it.' Daisy refills her glass, this time with a more generous measure. She looks at me. 'And Sam wouldn't cheat on me either.'

'You're not making sense. Sam has done it before. Men don't change, like you just so helpfully pointed out. If he's done it before, he could do it again. But it's worked for you, which gives me hope.'

'True, though that was years ago, and Sam was so young – he's a different person now. Plus we've had two children together, which has brought us closer. We've been through the hardest part.'

'You've told him about …?'

'Of course not.' Her face closes down for a second. 'That's strictly between us. I meant when the boys were really small. That was the hardest part. They're still a lot of work, but most of that is down to me because I'm at home with them. Sam earns a lot more than I do, and he works so hard I can't imagine he'd have time for an affair.'

Plus Daisy is pretty high maintenance. I'm sure she's right. I sigh.

'Look, I'm sorry for taking it out on you. The stuff with Theo is still pretty raw, no matter how much I try and pretend otherwise. And I'm not being fair to Sam. Coming back here to Blackwood reminds me of Hannah, and everything that happened. We've never really had closure, have we, so it's bound to.'

Daisy softens her voice. 'It's exactly the same for me, for all of us. Do you think I don't feel guilty about what happened? I hated myself for going behind her back with Sam, and he did too. But we fell in love – you must know what that's like – and surely the fact that we're still together today must count for something? It's proof that our feelings were real.'

I nod. 'I can see that now. At the time, I had never experienced being in love and I didn't think for a minute that you and Sam would last. Hannah didn't either, and she was my best friend and I had to take her side. Plus you and I have always rubbed each other up the wrong way, haven't we?'

Daisy smiles. 'Yes, but in a good way. And Amy will never stop trying to fix us.'

We sit in silence for a moment, the only sound in the room the quiet ticking of the clock in the hall. The atmosphere between us is shifting, changing, becoming less tense.

'Sam won't talk about it, you know.'

'The past?'

'Never has. I had to really work hard to persuade him to come this weekend. Once I convinced him the party was purely for Amy's birthday, he agreed.'

'But that's not strictly true, is it?'

'What do you mean?'

'Amy wants us to talk about what happened with Hannah, to put it to bed, as it were.'

'We'll have to do that before Saturday, then. The healing process is for us four, nobody else. The others will only be here for the Saturday evening, and that will be all about Amy.'

'Sam was a big part of it. It wasn't just us four.'

Despite my earlier misgivings it would actually help me if Sam was here. He and I need closure; I feel strongly that he should be part of it too. I won't push her, though. She'll take more notice if it comes from Amy, and I'm convinced Amy will want him here too.

'I'm glad we've had this chance to talk,' I say. 'I want to apologise for the way I behaved at the meal last time. It was before I'd found out about Theo's affair. Things were rocky between us and we'd argued about having children. You hit a sensitive subject, but you weren't to know. He knew I wanted to settle down and start a family, but he kept saying we should wait a while and I couldn't understand why. Now I can see it was because he was seeing someone else, but obviously I didn't know that at the time. That's why I reacted so badly to your remark about children. You hit a nerve, but you weren't to know.'

'I see. For a moment I thought you were going to blurt out about ...' That dark expression flits across her face again.

'I wouldn't do that. I promised you.'

'Just checking. Sam was furious. He said you didn't like me and he couldn't understand why you'd invited us. He was convinced you had it in for him because of Hannah. That's why he insisted we leave. He hadn't wanted to come in the first place.'

Snap. Nor had I.

'We go back a long way, me and you. Of course I don't dislike you. You've kept my confidence, after all, which proves I can trust you. Sometimes we clash, that's all – always have done. Let's try not to this weekend, for Amy's sake.'

'Sure,' Daisy says, and we clink glasses. For a second I consider telling her about my row with Hannah, letting go of the guilt I carry around with me, showing her we're not so different after all, but I'm not quite ready to trust her that far.

CHAPTER NINE

It's three in the morning when I wake. Darkness fills the sky and the cottage is shut down for the night. The happy fatigue I felt when I got into bed has been replaced by a tightness in my head and an unease in my stomach. The evening flashes through my mind: the pizzeria, Kat stomping up to bed, me clinking glasses with Daisy, anxiety about seeing Sam that morphs into thinking about Theo. Do I trust him, really, honestly? Can I ever get over that feeling?

The moment everything changed runs through my mind like a film reel. A normal Saturday. Theo had left for the gym and I'd stepped out from the shower wrapped in a towel, skin glowing, rested after a good night's sleep. The radio was playing, and I hummed along to a tune that I couldn't tell you the name of but had heard countless times before. I opened the wardrobe doors wide, wishing as I did every time that we had a wardrobe each instead of having to share, with my clothes squashed to the left and Theo's to the right. I selected a clean pair of jeans and a crisp white shirt. My navy blazer would go well with it but I couldn't find it amongst my jackets. Frowning, I double-checked and then went through Theo's side to see if it was there. As I did, my hands caught on a lanyard that was hanging out of one of Theo's jacket pockets. He must have forgotten it that morning. I would text him and let him know, in case he was worried he'd lost it. I tugged at the lanyard, and a tissue and a piece of pink paper fluttered to the floor: a Post-it note.

Love you.

How can two words cause so much pain?

I try to think about something else, and after managing to doze for a few hours, I creep out of bed and pull on my running gear, careful not to disturb Amy, who is sleeping deeply. Outside, I hear birdsong, and the sky is bright, the sun already high in the sky. The sound of my breath and my feet hitting the tarmac breaks into the silence. Forget the past; I have a future with Theo and I'm looking forward to seeing him on Saturday. Last weekend we drove out to the country for a long walk followed by a pub lunch. Over lunch, Theo suggested moving out of London and I spent the rest of the week in a state of excitement. Could I? The thought of leaving my job and my friends tugs at my heart, but the idea of buying a place in the country and settling down with Theo fills me with excitement. It feels like the right time to be starting a new phase.

My breathing is steady now as I run towards the town, the tiredness I felt on waking blown away. As I run, a light wind keeps my body temperature cool and I go over the conversation I had with Daisy, relieved that I've apologised for my behaviour at the meal, pleased we are back on track. Hopefully she'll update Sam. Just because we often clash, it doesn't lessen the strength of our friendship.

In the distance, colours flash – a row of painted front doors in a narrow street. When I reach the pink door of the first house, the shock of the Post-it note springs back into my head, and I turn and sprint, running as fast as I can with the wind behind me, feet stamping unwanted memories into the ground. He wants to have a baby with me and that's all that matters.

The light is on in the kitchen when I get back to the house. I leave my trainers at the back door and see Amy laying the table for breakfast. The smell of toast makes me feel suddenly ravenous.

'Amy, you're an angel. That smells heavenly.'

I fetch a glass of water and drink it in one go, taking in the welcome sight of the fresh bread, golden butter and strawberry jam set out on the table. The cafetière is filled and ready to plunge. The large clock on the wall tells me it's just after nine.

'I'm glad you think so. Daisy told me to go away when I woke her. Kat's up, though; I heard her in the shower. I wanted an early start to make the most of the time we have. I've got lots planned for today.'

'Such as?'

'I've booked a session on a climbing wall, followed by a steam room, then lunch.'

'Sounds great. What time?'

'Eleven. How did it go with Daisy last night?'

'Good, actually. We talked about the meal and it was a relief to clear the air. One thing I need to tell you, though: she wants us to talk about Hannah before Sam arrives on Saturday. She said he wouldn't have agreed to come otherwise.'

'But Sam is involved in this. If he's not there, we'll be missing a huge part of the jigsaw.'

'That's what I thought. I didn't say anything, though; it's better if you try and talk her round. She thinks I'm hard enough on Sam as it is.' He's always going to be a sticking point between us, but our friendship is important to me, and to Daisy too. 'As long as you're sure you want to get into it. It is your birthday, after all; wouldn't you rather concentrate on the future? Forget the past?'

Amy stops what she's doing, a pot of strawberry jam in her hand.

'I don't think that's possible. But if we think of it as an exorcism, it will do us all good. And you never know, it might raise some questions we should have been asking long ago. Trust me.'

I excuse myself to go off and shower, her words echoing in my head, mulling over the meaning. *Trust me.* If only I could. Life has taught me that the only person you can truly rely on is yourself. And exactly what questions does she mean? For a second I consider the possibility she might somehow know about me and Hannah, and a cold trickle runs down my spine.

Kat scales the climbing wall, hands and feet deftly placed, assured, lizard-like. Every now and then she stops to give encouragement to Daisy, who follows behind, her movements methodical, placing her hands extra carefully so as not to break her nails. Daisy would much rather be in a yoga class in her Lululemon gear with her own mat, no chance of germs, followed by matcha tea in an artisan café and a gossip with her friends. Hot and sweaty is not her style, but to her credit, she hasn't complained as much as we expected.

When the session is finished, Daisy looks pleased with herself. She's booked a full-body massage as a surprise for Amy. Kat and I opt for the steam room, and arrange to meet them afterwards. It's the perfect chance to have a talk with Kat, check everything is OK with Jade.

Heat envelops me as I step into a swirl of steam, the force of the atmosphere almost sending me straight back out. I stand still and wait for my body to adjust, squeeze my eyes shut until I feel more normal.

'Ooh, it's hot,' Kat says, adjusting the strap of her swimming costume as she moves through the steam. She climbs onto the higher level and lies down. I stretch out on the same level across from her. I'm happy to have this time with her. My skin prickles in the heat.

'You can't beat a steam room, can you?' Kat says, looking over at me. 'Especially after a good exercise session.'

'That hardly looked like exercise for you. You make everything seem so effortless. I enjoyed it, though. I let myself go a bit when all the stuff with Theo was going on, and now I'm making an effort to look after myself, get my body in tip-top condition.'

'It was a good idea, wasn't it? I think everyone is enjoying themselves. Good on Amy for getting us all together. It's about time. It would be cool if she could keep the cottage. It's a really sweet place.'

'Isn't it? It's not at all what I expected. I'd built it up in my head like the bogeyman's cottage in the wood.' Despite the heat in the steam room, a chill runs through me, and I adjust my position. 'I'm not sure she'd want to actually live so close to the forest, though.'

'That's what this weekend is all about. Making her feel good about being back here. And we've all got a part to play.'

'Did you find it hard to come back here? Honestly?'

'Yeah. I was secretly hoping it would be cancelled. Crap friend I am.'

'I was the same. We're lucky we don't have family ties to the area. It's harder for Amy because of her mum.'

'They live over the other side of town, though. Until recently, she had no need to come over to Blackwood.'

'Maybe her aunt left her the cottage for a reason.'

'I hadn't thought of that. Did Amy know her well?'

'She did when she was younger, but they lost contact around the time she finished her degree.'

'That makes sense, then, if they were close when Hannah disappeared. Leaving her the cottage could have been her aunt's way of helping her come to terms with what happened.'

'We'll have to ask her, when we actually sit down and discuss all this.'

Kat nods. Her forehead is perspiring and she wipes her face with a towel. 'I guess so. It won't be easy. Whenever I think about Hannah, I feel so guilty. I knew she wasn't happy and I didn't exactly help.'

'What do you mean?'

She wipes her face again. The steam makes a hissing noise.

'Kat?'

'Oh, nothing. I just wish I'd been there for her.'

'It's the same for all of us. Let's hope Amy's plan works.'

'It will change the dynamic if Sam is around. You and Daisy used to get on well, didn't you?'

'Really well. She used to confide in me a lot. We often had regular spats, but it was always forgotten the next time we saw each other. But after Sam came into the equation, we never quite reconciled. Taking Sam from Hannah was like kicking a puppy.'

'I wouldn't go that far. I wasn't surprised when they split.'

'Really? What makes you say that?' I lean up on my elbow. Kat is staring hard at the wall. She goes to speak, stops. Eventually she sits up.

'My gut. Speaking of which, I'm starving. Shall we go and get changed?'

I let it go, but wonder what she could have meant. Hannah and Sam never fought. What does Kat know that I don't?

Forty minutes later, we are showered and heading off to the café area. The corridor looks down over the badminton courts, where two men are involved in a game, and we pause for a moment to watch.

'That guy looks like Sam,' Kat says.

'He does,' I say as we carry on to the café.

Café is a bit of a grand description – it's four Formica tables and a vending machine humming in the corner, a large plastic dustbin overflowing with cans and bottles. It's empty apart from a woman drinking a can of lemonade. She's wearing a trench coat, which strikes me as strange attire.

I dump my bag on the table and sit down. Kat gets herself a bottle of water and drinks half of it in one go, her forehead creased in thought.

'When I first heard that Hannah had disappeared, I thought Sam had something to do with it, until we found out it was suicide.

Because he had a van, and somebody mentioned seeing her walking alongside a van.' She looks around the room before lowering her voice. 'For a horrible moment I'd assumed it was murder.'

Hannah went missing on a Monday. There was a lecture on the Brontës that afternoon, a particular interest of hers. We sat together halfway down the lecture theatre as we always did, cans of Coke in front of us, but instead of scribbling furiously all the way through as usual, she was distracted, eyes flitting from the lecturer to her lap, picking at the skin round her nails and barely writing a word. I asked her if she was all right, but she nodded without looking at me, jaw set. I assumed she was still upset about Sam and Daisy. I couldn't concentrate either. My heart ached for her and I wished there was something I could do to make her feel better. Towards the end of the lecture, she kept looking at her watch, and the moment it was finished, she muttered that she had an appointment. Ordinarily we'd stroll back to our hall together, but nothing about Hannah had been ordinary since the split with Sam, which had devastated her. That was the last time I ever saw her.

She wasn't reported missing until the following morning. The story hit the local news that day, and a televised appeal went out two days later. Amy and I watched it on the small television screen in her room. An article in the newspaper the next day reported that several members of the public had rung in following the appeal with information, and the police were currently working through it. The only new piece of information they released was that she had been seen walking alongside a van. Sam had a white van, but I pushed the thought from my mind.

Hannah's body was found in Blackwood Forest the following day. I wasn't able to look Sam in the eye the next time we met, fearing he could sense that I had doubted him, even if only for a moment. It was my fault our relationship hadn't recovered after that. It would be good to rectify my error of judgement and resume our friendship when he arrived. Daisy and Sam had been married for years, and it was time for me to make my peace with him. I had always wondered, though, whether it was just me who had had that sneaking suspicion about him.

'So you suspected Sam? Even if just for a moment?' If I wasn't the only one, I'd feel better about having those thoughts.

'It crossed my mind, of course it did. Mostly because of the van, which is a crap reason really – thousands of people drive vans. But once he'd been questioned and released, I figured that if the police were happy, then so was I. Besides, I didn't think he had it in him. He did love Hannah for a long time. And then of course it was all redundant when we found out the awful truth. But Sam's not so bad,' she adds. 'After all, he's put up with Daisy and her exacting standards for all these years. They've certainly proved all their doubters wrong.' She drinks some more water. 'Why? Is it still bothering you? I thought you said you'd …' She stops mid sentence, looking over my shoulder. I turn to see Daisy and Amy standing behind us.

'Good massage?' Kat says.

'It was just what I needed,' Amy replies, but Daisy is looking between me and Kat. How long have they been standing there? Surely they can only just have arrived, or Kat would have seen them earlier. 'I almost fell asleep.'

'What about you, Daisy?' Kat says.

'Yeah, it was good. Relaxing.' Daisy tightens her grip on her bag, which is slung over her shoulder.

'The steam room was lovely,' I say.

'No doubt you had a good old chat.' She pauses. 'It looked like we were interrupting something just now.'

'We were only wondering where we might be going for lunch. I've worked up an almighty appetite.'

'OK,' Daisy says, though the way she narrows her eyes tells me she doesn't believe me. But why would I tell Kat her secret now, after all this time?

As we leave the café, the woman in the trench coat watches us. She must be waiting for someone.

We have just reached the car park when Daisy's phone rings.

'Sam,' she mouths, and wanders away from the car. We all get in and wait for her.

'Bloody man,' she says, striding back, her face flushed and her hair blown out of place in the breeze. 'He's going to be late. He promised me he would only work in the morning and would get here early Saturday afternoon.'

'I'm sure he didn't do it deliberately,' Amy says. 'What time will he arrive?'

'He doesn't know. Late afternoon, I hope.' She brushes her hair away from her face with an irritated sweep of her hand. 'And don't be so reasonable, Amy, he doesn't deserve it.'

Amy starts the ignition and reverses the car.

'Am I all right to pull out?' she asks.

I swivel round to look through the back windscreen.

'Yes, all clear.'

Amy pulls out, but I can't take my eyes from the window. The woman from the café is standing outside the doors of the leisure centre, her gaze fixed on our car. As we drive away, she notes something down in her phone. Goosebumps prickle the back of my neck.

CHAPTER TEN

Amy proposes three potential lunch places and we opt for a tiny Turkish cafe. We order a shared mezze, which arrives in a glorious array of colour and aromas. Every table is occupied, and chatter vies with the music playing through speakers in the ceiling. The cheerful atmosphere pushes thoughts of the woman from my mind. Being back in Blackwood is making my imagination go wild.

'I'd forgotten how busy the town centre is,' I say, loading my plate with stuffed vine leaves, hummus and warm flatbread, which smells slightly burnt and delicious. 'What's the plan for the rest of the day?'

'Please, no more activities. Can't we just chill out in the garden with a bottle of wine?' Daisy says.

Amy laughs. 'No more activities, I promise. We'll pick up some food after lunch, then go back home. I'm cooking tonight, and that's basically it. The rest is up to you. Chilling out in the garden sounds like a great idea.'

'And what exactly is the plan for the party?' Kat tops up the water glasses from the carafe on the table.

'It's only us,' Amy says. 'I went through loads of ideas of ways to spend my thirty-fifth – which in case you're wondering is a milestone worth celebrating when you've had the year I've had. I'm not waiting until my fortieth for the next big bash. You got off lightly today actually, Daisy; at one point I was considering a bungee jump, but in the end, all I wanted was to be with my oldest friends. I know we haven't stayed in touch as I would have liked, but I still feel close to you all because those three years were so intense. And "party" is perhaps rather a grand way to describe tomorrow. There will be food and music and conversation, and' – she drinks some water – 'I also wanted for us to be able to remember Hannah in some way.'

'We guessed as much,' Kat says. 'But how exactly?'

'I thought we could talk about her, share memories, I don't know … Don't you ever wonder what she would have been like now? How she would have turned out?'

I nod. 'She'd most likely be a professor specialising in the Brontës, living the full Yorkshire experience with her dogs.'

'Looking gorgeous at the same time,' Amy adds.

'With a family of adorable children and a handsome husband.'

Kat says, 'She might have had a really hard life and ended up homeless.'

Daisy rolls her eyes. 'That was never going to happen. There's no need to be so extreme, Kat. OK, she was having a hard time after splitting from her first boyfriend and was struggling with her finals, but she'd have got over it. She'd be married with children, you could tell; she was that type of woman.'

'We'll never know,' Amy says, 'and that's the whole point of this. I want to stop wondering and celebrate her for how we remember her. Do you think Sam will be OK with that? I'd like him to be there.'

'If I tell him, he definitely won't come. But what you're suggesting sounds like a really nice idea. Once it's happening, he'll be fine, I'm sure.' Daisy laughs. 'If I'm OK with it, then he will be too.'

We all nod in agreement. I wonder if the others feel the same sense of foreboding that has taken hold of me.

'Thanks for arranging this, Amy,' I say. 'It helps a lot. I can't say I'm exactly happy to be back here, but you know, what I would like to do, sometime this weekend, is to make some kind of gesture. Maybe visit the place where Hannah was found. It would help me draw a line under it all in some way. It's been years since I went there, and I'd like to lay some flowers.' With her having been buried back near her parents, this is the next best thing.

'Could do,' Kat says.

'Isn't that a bit morbid? I get that we want to remember her, but really? That forest is creepy at the best of times.' Daisy shudders dramatically.

'I think we should,' Amy says. 'We need to stop seeing the forest as a place of horror. Inheriting the cottage has made me want to face up to my fears. If I'd just sold it, we wouldn't be here now, doing this. I'm half wondering whether that's the reason my aunt left it to me: to help me make peace with what happened.'

'How funny,' Kat says. 'We were talking about that earlier.'

'She saw the state I was in at the time. It's important, I think. If we don't all go, it won't be the same. I'd like you to come with us. Daisy.'

'Fine, I'm not fussed either way, but not this afternoon, please. I'd really like to get back to the house and chill out. Not having the children is such a rare occurrence for me, and I want to make the most of just being able to think about myself for once.'

We decide that Kat and I will do the shopping while the others go back to the cottage.

'It's so strange being back here, don't you think?' Kat says, as we pack the groceries into the hessian bag Amy gave us.

'It is,' I say. 'But I'm glad we came.' The town conjures up good memories of discovering it for the first time as a fresher, enjoying the respite from campus.

She nods. 'Me too. It's nice to escape from the hustle and bustle once in a while. Let's get a coffee from that van, sit in the sun for a bit before we go back.'

It was always my intention to come back to Blackwood, but somehow I could never make myself do it. If it wasn't for Amy, it would probably never have happened. I'm glad she's done this, forced us all to face up to the past.

Kat brings two coffees over to the empty bench I've nabbed for us. I pick up our earlier conversation.

'What you were saying before, about Sam, and the van; for me that was compounded by the way he treated Hannah, dumping her for Daisy. Didn't that bother you too?'

Kat shrugs. 'At the time, a bit, but in hindsight not at all. Sam was Hannah's first boyfriend – you don't expect your first relationship to last, do you? Yes, it was full-on drama at the time, but Daisy's right, Hannah would have moved on by now.' She laughs. 'Thank God I'm not still mooning around after Alison Postlethwaite.'

'You liked Alison Postlethwaite? You kept that quiet.'

'And wouldn't you? I was desperately in love with her. It killed me when she started dating that moron from the history department. I can't even remember his name.'

'Greg something … Sutherland, that was it.'

'Yes, him. Acne Greg, I used to call him. Poor git. He was covered in spots yet she preferred him to me. Story of my life. What I'm saying is the whole thing seems worlds away. Sometimes, just sometimes, these things last, and you can't deny Daisy and Sam have had a pretty good innings.'

I change the subject. 'What's going on with Jade, Kat?'

She draws a pattern on the floor with her foot.

'I've no idea. When I have, I'll tell you.'

Daisy is lazing on an orange sunlounger when we get back to the cottage. It's covered in thick cotton material in a swirly flower pattern, and the colour has faded where the sun has burned into the fabric. A bottle of sunscreen is on the ground beside her, and her face is covered with a magazine. Amy is sitting in the shade on a striped deckchair, and two more folded chairs are leaning against the shed. She looks up from her paperback when we come in through the side gate.

'What a lovely afternoon,' I say.

'Isn't it? These chairs are the best I could find in the shed. You should have seen the cobwebs when we dug them out. Daisy insisted on wiping them all down. Comfy, are you, Daisy?'

'I'm asleep,' Daisy says.

Kat and I unfold the deckchairs and join them.

'I told Kat about the podcast,' I say to Amy.

She looks at me. 'I haven't decided whether I want to get involved yet. I wanted to see how this weekend panned out first.'

'The mental health angle is a good one, and it's very high-profile at the moment,' I say.

'And so it should be.' Kat nods. 'For far too long there's been a stigma attached to it. Take Hannah's situation. Did any of you know she had been suffering from depression? We all knew she was devastated by her split with Sam, but we assumed she'd get over it eventually. I think there was more to it, though, that her feelings went far deeper.'

'I did.' Daisy hasn't moved, her face still covered. 'Sam told me she'd had treatment when she was at school. It wasn't all me. Living with her was difficult when she was struggling.'

'Really?' I say. Hannah never mentioned that to me. 'I had no idea and she was my closest friend. We talked a lot, and I encouraged her to see the doctor on campus, who referred her for counselling. How did I not know that she'd been treated for depression?'

'We can't beat ourselves up about it,' Amy says. 'It's always easy in hindsight to see what should have been done, but actually, we did all we could.'

'If someone is determined to die by suicide, if they're that unhappy, I don't think anyone can stop them. It's like addiction. Only the addict can help themselves.' Daisy sits up and drinks some water. 'I'm not sure I'd want to be involved in a podcast. It's slightly different for me, given my profile. I'd have to take advice from my agent.'

Amy nods. 'It will be harrowing, there's no doubt about that. But if it serves a wider purpose and gets the message out there, it could really help others.'

'Do you know if her family are on board?' Kat asks. 'It would be up to them in the first instance. I doubt they'd want it all dredged up again.'

'Jonathan – that's the name of the journalist – said they hadn't given him a definitive answer yet. They might see it as a way of preventing other young people going through the same thing.'

'I don't want to be involved,' Kat says.

I'm surprised; Kat's usually the first to champion a cause. All her artwork is related to women and the struggle to be equal, each sculpture carrying its own message.

'I doubt it will happen anyway,' Amy says. 'I've got other priorities.'

'Yes, like finding Mr Right,' I say. 'We'll get you signed up to Bumble.' I take out my phone.

'Bumble? What's that?'

'It's a dating site, dummy,' Kat says. 'Even I've heard of it and I've never been on a blind date in my life.'

'It's not a blind date as such,' I say, frowning at her. I don't want her to put Amy off. 'You get the opportunity to get to know someone before you commit to anything. And it's up to the woman to reach out first, so you don't get harassed like on some sites.' I glance at the others. 'Amy's ready to date again, aren't you, Amy?'

'I suppose so,' she says, looking at my phone as though it's a loaded weapon.

'You can't chicken out now. Let's set up a profile.'

Kat scrolls through the photos on Amy's phone to find a suitable one while I help her create a profile.

'Yesterday you said looks don't matter, right?'

'Hang on. That doesn't mean I haven't got standards. Of course looks matter to a certain extent. But we need to have lots of shared interests. That was another area that didn't work with Phil. He used to spend hours watching golf on the television.'

'Crikey,' Kat says. 'That's bad. No golf, Lou, top priority. Any other pet hates?'

'Yes. No sense of humour. Humour is high on my list.'

'That's a given,' I say. 'All you have to do now is fill in the questionnaire and you're good to go.'

'Excellent.' Amy groans. 'Do I really have to answer all these questions? "How would you rate your energy levels? What is your ideal Sunday morning? How would you rate your success at work?" Really? This is worse than a job application.'

'Of course you do,' I say, closing my eyes and enjoying the sun on my face. 'How else will they be able to match you?'

She puts her phone down.

'Hey, you haven't found Mr Right yet,' Kat says.

'I've made a step in the right direction. That's all you're getting for today.'

'We'll get you swiping right before the end of this weekend, won't we, Lou?'

'We certainly will.' A breeze ripples through the garden, and I shiver. Hannah thought she'd found her Mr Right, and look how she ended up.

Blackwood Independent, 28 April 2005

Missing university student Hannah Robinson was upset after breaking up with her boyfriend of almost three years, a close friend has said. The outstanding student, on course for a first-class degree in English, had been under a lot of stress prior to her disappearance, and had sought advice from the campus doctor. Friends of the reserved but popular student insist she was coping, despite going through a difficult time with her finals looming, and would never have disappeared of her own volition. Hannah's family endorse this view and implore their daughter to get in touch. The student has been missing for three days now, and her friends and family are increasingly worried.

CHAPTER ELEVEN

'Thanks for organising this, Amy,' Kat says, after popping open the bottle of champagne I surprised them with and filling our glasses, along with some sparkling elderflower for me. 'And why not?' she says when Amy tells her she shouldn't have. 'It's a special occasion. Look at you, resplendent on the eve of your thirty-fifth birthday.'

She's right. We're all sitting around the dining table, a tall candle in the centre, the room lit by two lamps. The lasagne has been served; bowls of salad and bread sit in the middle of the table. The soft lighting picks out copper-coloured highlights in Amy's freshly washed hair, and her curls bounce on her shoulders whenever she moves. The red jumpsuit she's wearing has tiny silver flecks in the fabric that shimmer in the light, and it matches her trademark red lipstick. An urge to cry at seeing her look so well overcomes me, and I swallow it down.

'To Amy.' Kat raises her glass, and we all follow suit.

'To Amy.'

Amy's eyes fill with tears and I'm glad it's not just me who's moved by this.

An image comes to mind of the six of us crammed into her university room, eighteen-year-olds with one tentative foot on the rung of the ladder of adult life. Full of hopes, dreams, desires. I wondered about them, those other students who'd taken exactly the same path as me, chosen that university, at that particular time. Did they feel as I did, that we were embarking on a huge adventure and there would be no going back? Later, I'd find out that for Kat, a university miles from her home town was a chance to escape her miserable home life. Amy had a passion for English and literature, was eager for knowledge. Daisy's determination to be on the stage had started at the age of six, when she was cast as a rogue sheep in an innovative primary school pantomime and had apparently stolen the show. Naturally. Once I got to know her, I realised it couldn't be any other way. The combined theatre studies degree was a way of appeasing her parents before applying to the top drama schools in the country. And Hannah … Hannah wanted more than anything to be loved, she told me once we'd got to know one another. A stepbrother she didn't get on with and older parents who weren't very demonstrative meant she was looking for warmth, companionship. I was yet to learn all this about these women who were to become my firm friends. All thanks to Amy.

'If it wasn't for Amy, we might never have met,' I say. 'Do you remember that first evening?' The memory sticks in my mind as if it were yesterday, and I wonder if it does in theirs too. If events hadn't panned out as they did, would the moment be frozen in time like this?

'Of course,' Daisy says. 'How could we forget?'

The image is vivid in my mind. Amy had asked us all round for tea and cakes one midweek afternoon. Hannah and I arrived last, and I squeezed onto the bed along with Daisy and Amy. Kat took the chair at the desk and Hannah had no choice but to sit on the floor next to Sam. Tall and slim in a simple white T-shirt and blue jeans, she folded herself neatly into the space next to him, her long, straight fair hair tickling his arm as she did so. She flicked it back over her shoulder as she spoke her first words to him, and didn't move from the spot all night.

Afternoon tea ran into evening drinks, bottles of wine and cans of beer were brought in from the kitchen, and Sam and Hannah chatted and laughed as if they'd known each other for ages. I was delighted, seeing quiet Hannah opening up like a blossoming flower. She wasn't flirting and preening, though; everything she did always seemed so natural. I'd warmed to Sam immediately for his easy-going manner, putting Hannah at ease.

Everyone seemed comfortable, relaxed in each other's company, despite all being quite different. There was glamorous Daisy with her painted fingernails, her elegant manners and her loud voice, which commanded attention; she was the kind of person everybody had seen around campus and we appreciated her coolness. It was no surprise to anyone when she was one of the few from the theatre department who went on to make it big on television. Kat in an oversize denim shirt and combat trousers, with spiky dark hair and a wicked sense of humour. Amy was wearing a long dress with big red flowers all over it, her perfectly lipsticked mouth matching the colour, all set off by a green bow, and she oozed delight at seeing her disparate group of friends coming together.

It was that day that cemented my decision to stay in Buckinghamshire. Up until that point I hadn't been sure – I was enjoying the course, but I missed my friends from home and even found myself missing Mum and Dad. By the end of that evening, I'd found my tribe.

'You might not remember this, Lou,' Amy says, 'but you were quite tipsy when you left …'

'We all were,' Daisy says, 'I spent the whole of the next day in bed.'

'How can you remember so far back?' Kat shakes her head. 'I can barely remember what I was doing last week.'

'As I was saying.' Amy raises her voice, commanding attention. 'Lou threw her arms around me at the end and whispered how much she loved my friends and could they be her friends too.'

'Yes, it was hysterical,' Kat says, 'because she thought she was whispering quietly.'

'Ha!' Daisy says. 'It was more like a stage whisper, penetrating every corner of the room. We all heard it. Even Hannah and Sam.'

She rolls her eyes, and I wonder if she's recalling the moment Sam reached out to move a strand of Hannah's hair from her face, and how oblivious to the rest of us they appeared.

'It was sweet,' Amy says quickly, pretending not to hear the edge in Daisy's tone. 'Obviously I said yes. And it's funny how you quickly became the one we all turned to for advice.'

She's right: back then, all four of them said they found me so easy to talk to – Sam too – though that was before Daisy's betrayal of Hannah. I experience a pang of loss, followed by a twist of alarm, as I recall the secret I've always kept for Daisy, even now.

I watch as she laughs along with the rest of us, but she's gripping her glass tightly and her smile is the kind you fix on your face for an unwelcome photograph. It can't be easy for her, the memory of that evening, because the one thing we always used to talk about whenever we thought back to it prior to the final year was how Hannah and Sam were so obviously meant to be together, the way they'd gravitated to one another and not let go. Until Daisy set her sights on him.

She had flirted with him right from the start, but then Daisy was programmed to flirt with all men, so none of us thought anything of it. It's unfortunate for her that what happened with Sam has grown in importance because of Hannah's disappearance; if Hannah had lived, she would have moved on, and who knows, maybe she'd be here with us now, her partner arriving on Saturday with the others, greeting Sam like the old friend he'd become. But that picture wobbles and fades, and somehow I know it isn't the right image. Hannah would never have forgotten Sam; it was one of those kinds of loves. Real, enduring love.

I'm being sentimental, and I can't even blame the champagne. I shake the image from my mind and bring myself back to what Kat is saying.

'And it's thanks to you again, Ames, that we've all come together this weekend. I can't believe it's the first time in … how many years?'

'Fourteen,' Daisy says without having to pause and work it out like I'm doing in my head. 'But it's not as if we haven't been in touch. Amy and I message each other often, and Louise and I met up last year. It's only Kat I haven't seen for a while.'

'Louise and I have seen each other quite a bit, but it's easier us both being in London,' Kat says. 'I'm sorry, you guys, it's my fault. You know what a workaholic I am. I get so busy sometimes I forget to feed myself, let alone call my friends.'

'And there's the small matter of your girlfriend … This must be The One for you, eh, Kat?' Daisy asks. 'You've been together for how long now?'

'A while,' Kat says. 'But that's no excuse. Thankfully Amy has kept us updated about each other, so we've never lost touch completely. It's all down to you, Amy. Such a loyal friend.'

'And so have you all been, especially during the last couple of years,' Amy says. Her mouth wobbles and her eyes fill with tears. Her champagne glass bears a bright red smudge on the rim.

'Stop it,' Daisy says. 'No crying. This weekend is all about celebration. It's our duty to make sure you have a fabulous time. Pass the champagne, Kat.'

'There's none left. I'll open some wine.'

When their glasses are filled, Amy clears her throat. 'Of course we're going to have a fabulous time, as you put it, Daisy, but I'd like us all to address the elephant in the room. I believe if she'd still been alive Hannah would have been part of this group, here with us now, and I'd like us to remember her this weekend, talk about what happened, because I think it will help us. We can't change her story, and we'll never know what made her so unhappy that she chose to take her own life, but let's say a proper goodbye to her. We never got the chance back then, with everything that happened. You lot all went elsewhere and I was the only one left behind. I know it hasn't been easy, coming back here, but thank you for making the effort. Lou's idea to visit the place where they found her is perfect, and I'd like to do that.'

Even though it was my idea, the skin at the back of my neck prickles at the thought of Blackwood Forest, the narrow path surrounded by brambles on one side and stinging nettles on the other. The small clearing where her body was found, laid out like a swastika after she'd fallen, her eyes looking up to the square of grey sky visible through the treetops. A crow could be heard up high.

'Like I said, it would be nice to take some flowers, mark the spot in some way,' I say. 'It will make us feel better.'

'You're implying we're all feeling bad about Hannah somehow,' Daisy says, sipping her wine. Tiny red stains mark the sides of her mouth, like horns.

'Well, aren't we? Isn't that what this is all about? Facing up to our demons?' Kat is facing the candle, and the breath behind her words causes the flame to flicker violently. 'Hannah's death was like a rocket shooting into our little group and blowing it apart. I used to love living here, I'd planned to stay in the area, but after her disappearance, I couldn't wait to get away.'

Amy stops eating and picks up her wine glass, takes a sip before speaking.

'Kat's right; that's exactly why I invited you all. To mend the hole that Hannah's death caused. I've wanted to visit the spot in the forest for ages, but couldn't face it alone. Let's go tomorrow morning. Or should we wait, so that Sam can come too?'

'You're joking,' Daisy says. 'Sam needed persuading just to come back here at all. The police treated him horribly at the time. It was awful for him.'

'He'd been dating Hannah, so clearly he was a person of interest,' I say. 'You know they always suspect those closest to a victim. We were all on their radar until they realised what had happened,' I say.

'They persecuted him.' Daisy's eyes flash as bright as the candlelight. 'That's why he stayed in his room all the time, only came out for his exams.'

'We can't change the past,' Kat says. 'I just wish we could have stopped her.'

'There was something wrong with her,' I say slowly, 'and if only we knew what that was, I'm sure it would take us closer to understanding why she did it. For months she hadn't been herself – and this started before she stopped going out with Sam, so it's not your fault, Daisy; her defences were down and that just made her feel worse. Something was bugging her and she wouldn't talk about it. I'm sure it was more concrete than depression.'

'I honestly never noticed,' Kat says. 'Shows what a crap friend I am.'

'Or maybe she just had a problem with you, Louise,' Daisy says. For a second I think she knows; but Hannah would never have told her. I try to convince myself she's merely defending Sam like I always defend Theo, blaming his affair on the other woman.

My cheeks burn at the memory of that one time I lost my temper with Hannah. Everything comes back to her. Emotions run like wildfire through my system when I think about her suicide and her wasted life, the guilt I felt after my argument with Hannah, my confusion about what had happened rumbling under the surface.

'Maybe she did,' I say, 'but if that's true, I wish I'd known what it was. Maybe then I could have prevented what happened.'

Amy rubs my arm. 'Stop blaming yourself,' she says. 'Although I think we're all doing that. It will do us good to go to the forest and pay our respects to Hannah. And when we're there, we should each of us make our peace, stop blaming ourselves and each other. What do you think, Daisy?'

'Sure, as long as we go before the others arrive, keep Sam out of it. He just doesn't have the same emotional response as we do.'

'He's a guy,' Kat says. 'I agree, Amy. I reckon it will do us all good.'

'Excellent,' Amy says. 'Now, enough of that. I want to talk about being thirty-five and discuss what to do about my secret grey hairs.'

'And we can find you some matches on Bumble,' Daisy says.

'There is one guy I quite liked the look of,' Amy admits.

How easily they dismiss the conversation. I wish I could compartmentalise my life like that. My stomach churning from our discussion, I push my plate to one side, the lasagne congealing, the tomato sauce dried in a trail of red.

CHAPTER TWELVE

My forehead is slick with sweat when I wake, heart hammering from running through the forest, desperate to leave my unknown assailant behind, needing to find Hannah and warn her. My feet get tangled with a twisted tree root and I'm falling, opening my eyes when I hit the floor. My face is buried in the pillow. I lie still until my pulse returns to normal. It's been a while since I've had the dream, but I'm not surprised it has returned this weekend. If I sit up in bed, I can see the forest treetops in the near distance.

Downstairs, the kitchen is still, and I close the back door quietly, fitting in a thirty-minute run before getting back to make breakfast. It's to be a treat for Amy, who's gone to such trouble to organise this weekend break for us. I pick some daffodils from the garden and arrange them in a glass jug, which I set on the table, on the white cotton tablecloth I find in one of the drawers. Amy prefers tea, so I make a pot of Earl Grey in the bright red teapot that reminds me of my grandma, who had an identical one in blue. Her tea was always served with a fat home-made Victoria sponge cake whenever I went to visit. By the time Daisy comes in yawning, the table is laden with a loaf of bread, cereals, jam, butter and juice. I can't help thinking about Sam, wish I didn't always feel that flutter of anxiety that follows the thoughts.

'Morning,' I say. 'Perfect timing. Are the others up yet?'

She stretches her arms overhead and gives an exaggerated yawn. 'I heard Amy moving about.'

'I'll go and check. Help yourself to tea if you want.'

Kat grunts from her bed when I tap at her door, and Amy has just got out of the shower.

'Happy birthday,' I say.

'Cheers,' she says, hitching up her towel.

'How does it feel to be thirty-five?'

'Same as yesterday.'

We both laugh. 'Breakfast is ready when you are.'

'Great.'

'You OK?' I ask.

She nods. 'Half asleep. I need tea.'

'Coming up.'

Daisy is slumped at the kitchen table where I left her.

'Sleep well?' I ask as I push down the plunger in the cafetière.

She stretches her legs out under the table. 'I did. Despite Kat's snoring. And it was bliss not to be woken at a ridiculous hour. Alfie always gets up before six and still thinks it's hilarious to jump on me when I'm asleep – never his dad, for some reason – then refuses to go downstairs and play without me. He beseeches me with his big blue eyes and I fall for it every time.'

'Here's a coffee to make up for it.' I place the mug in front of her. Kat appears in the doorway, yawning.

'Morning,' she says. 'Ooh, coffee, just what I need.' She holds up a present wrapped in gold paper and puts it on the table.

'Coming up,' I say. 'Do you want toast?'

'No thanks, just coffee. Did we all sleep all right?' She sits opposite Daisy.

'Yes, apart from you snoring,' Daisy says.

Kat puts her hands up. 'You get to share a room with me, it's part of the package. Some people would pay good money to hear me snore.' She clutches the mug as if it's giving her strength and drinks some coffee. 'Hmm, that's better. Anyone know what Amy's got in store for us today?'

'Something non-physical, I hope,' Daisy says.

Nobody mentions the visit to the forest. Maybe they're all having second thoughts. It's important to me, and I'm determined to go even if I end up doing so alone. But to go as a group would feel like an important step forward.

'Morning,' Amy says. Kat jumps up and gives her a hug.

'Happy birthday.'

'Thanks. The flowers are a nice touch. And the table looks lovely. Was that you, Lou?'

I nod. 'Tea? I'll be mother for once.'

'Yes please.'

Ten minutes later, we're all eating toast, except for Daisy, who's opted for granola, yogurt and fresh strawberries. Amy is delighted with the turquoise and gold scarf we've given her. Kat spreads a thick layer of peanut butter on her toast.

'You don't know how good this is,' Daisy says, giving a satisfied sigh. 'Although an extra hour in bed would have made it perfect. Breakfast in our house is normally squabbles over Coco Pops and milk splashed on clean clothes. Usually mine. Sam always leaves early so misses out on the pleasure of family breakfast. Some days I can't wait to get back to work.'

'My breakfast usually involves several cups of coffee,' Kat says. 'I get straight down to work as soon as I wake, as the light in my studio is better in the morning. Then I have a kind of brunch at lunchtime. It often involves pancakes. What's the plan for today?'

'I suggest we go to the forest this morning,' Amy says.

'Get it out of the way, you mean.'

'Daisy! Last night you said it was good idea.'

'Did I? I must have been drunk. I'd just rather do it before the others arrive this afternoon.' Her phone rings. 'Talk of the devil, it's Sam. I'll take it outside.' She picks it up and goes out into the garden.

'She didn't drink that much last night, did she?'

'Ignore her, she's just making excuses. She won't want to stay here alone,' Kat says, crunching into her toast.

Daisy's raised voice can be heard outside. I get up, ostensibly to make more coffee, but stand where I can see her. She's pacing round the lawn having an energetic conversation, but she's scowling when she comes back in.

'What's up?' Amy asks. 'Don't say he's not coming after all.'

Until that moment I hadn't realised I was tensing my shoulders. They relax at the thought that Sam might not be coming. It would be so much easier for me if he weren't here. Finally, I've admitted it to myself.

'He's coming, but he's going to be even later than he said. I'm absolutely bloody furious. He promised me he would leave at lunchtime. He's like this every weekend. It's the boys I feel bad for. They hardly ever get to see him because he works so bloody hard. I just don't understand it.'

'How late is he going to be?'

She shrugs. 'No idea. He's ringing me later. He couldn't even give me an estimate.'

I'm not really surprised to hear this; Sam was clearly already reluctant to come back here. *What if he doesn't want to see me?* He could be as anxious as I am. I sip my coffee, wincing at the bitter taste. Has Daisy realised that too? Will she take it out on me? *Stop.* I promised myself I wouldn't do this. Daisy's making an effort and so must I.

Amy goes upstairs to the bathroom.

'Come on, Daisy, we mustn't let anything spoil today, for Amy's sake,' Kat says. 'You said yourself you didn't want Sam to go to the forest, so now he won't have to. I'm sure he'll be here by the time we get back.'

'Maybe,' she says, but she pushes her uneaten granola aside.

*

By the time we all bundle into Amy's car, Daisy has cheered up. She sits in the front chatting to Amy, while Kat and I are in the back.

'Have you heard from Jade today?' I ask Kat.

'No.'

'Is she coming tonight?'

'Probably not,' she says, turning away from me, her lips pressed together. For the rest of the journey she gazes out of the window. Normally she's so talkative, making a joke of her problems. This has to be more serious. Is being back here getting to her too?

Amy parks in the car park and retrieves the flowers we bought in town from the boot of the car. White roses and yellow tulips.

'Do you know where exactly to go?' Kat asks.

Amy nods and leads us towards a path at the end of the car park. Daisy stops when we get to it.

'Look at the mud. Do you really expect me to walk in that?'

'What's the problem? You're wearing trainers.'

'They're new.'

'You knew we were coming to the forest,' Kat says, looking at Daisy's pristine white pumps. She lopes along the path behind Amy with her normal energetic stride.

'Yes, but I didn't realise it had rained last night. I was dead to the world once my head hit the pillow.'

'Ha. I knew you were lying about my snoring.'

We walk in single file as a couple approach with a dog bounding ahead of them. Daisy stops to stroke it.

'The boys want a puppy,' she says, 'but I've told them they'll have to wait until they're old enough to look after it. Otherwise I know it will all be left down to me.'

For the first time it occurs to me that Daisy and Sam might be having problems themselves. She's mentioned more than once the amount of time he spends at work, how he's never home much for the children; and there's the argument they had earlier. Relationships can be such hard work, and Daisy herself isn't easy.

I watch Amy, ahead of me. She hasn't had a relationship since she split with Phil. So many times during the last year, when she's been going through such a tough time, I've wished she had a partner to support her, but on the other hand, she hasn't had to put up with the crap side of relationships, like finding out your partner is shagging someone else. The memory of the pink Post-it note flutters into my head, and I run to catch up with her and away from my thoughts.

Amy comes to a halt and we all stop behind her. Over her shoulder we can see the clearing. My head feels light and I step back and let the others take a look first. Hannah's world ended here. The trees around me feel oppressive, with their broad trunks and huge branches that block the sunlight from our path. I drink some water from the bottle in my bag and re-join the others.

'What's that?' Daisy asks as we move forward, pointing at something over by the tree where Hannah was found. A distinctive-looking log lies at the base of the trunk, which was how we'd always managed to remember the exact spot.

'It's a bunch of flowers,' Kat says. 'Who would have put those there?' She kneels down to inspect them. 'No note with them.'

'Her family, I suppose.'

Amy lays our flowers next to the pink roses, and we stand in a horseshoe shape, looking down at the spot. The clearing is silent save for birdsong.

'Let's have a minute's silence for Hannah,' Amy says, and we all hold hands.

I close my eyes, wishing I knew exactly what happened on that fateful day. What was Hannah feeling in those final moments? Was she really without hope, or were more sinister forces at play? The thought makes my skin go cold.

Amy drops my hand as a sign that the minute is up, and we all remain still, like the trees around us, lost in our thoughts. A twig cracks loudly, and I look in the direction it came from.

88　　　　　　　　　LESLEY SANDERSON

'What was that?' I move away from the flowers, Kat following me. Something catches my eye in the bushes to the left, a flash of beige. 'Did you see that?'

'What?' She looks in the direction I'm pointing.

'I'm sure I saw somebody.'

Kat moves closer to the bushes, then beckons me over. 'Look, there's a woman over there. She can't see us as that tree is in the way, but she's watching Amy and Daisy. Can you see her?'

I move to the side and see a woman in a beige trench coat bending at what looks like an uncomfortable angle. My pulse speeds up. It's the woman from the leisure centre.

A twig cracks under my foot, and she starts and looks over. When she sees us approaching her, she looks surprised, but she quickly changes her expression before walking towards us. My pulse goes up another notch.

'Hello,' she says, holding out her hand to Kat, who is the nearer of the two of us. Kat looks at her hand, then at her face.

'Can we help you?' she asks. 'You seem rather interested in our friends.'

'Jules Barker,' the woman says. '*Blackwood Independent*. I'm looking into the case of Hannah Robinson, whose body was found at this spot fourteen years ago. Given the flowers, I'm assuming you were friends of hers.'

'Did you leave those flowers?' I ask.

She nods. 'It seemed appropriate. Am I right? Did you know her?'

'Case? What case?' Kat says.

Amy and Daisy come over to join us, dead leaves crackling under their feet.

'What's going on?' Daisy asks.

'I'm Jules Barker, *Blackwood Independent*. It's the local newspaper,' she adds, in case we don't know it. But we do. How could we ever forget? The few stories the paper ran during those last months we were living here were like a drug. I'd pore over every line, desperate for the tiniest snippet of information about Hannah.

'We know the newspaper,' Kat says.

'You're all local, then? I haven't seen you around.'

'We're visiting for the weekend.'

The journalist flashes a look at the four of us, trying to gauge our mood, how much to say. Amy steps forward and offers her hand.

'Amy Barnes. I went to university with Hannah. We all did.'

'Jules,' the woman says again. 'I'm looking into the case.'

'I'm not sure what you mean by that. Hannah killed herself; she isn't a case, or a statistic. She was a lovely human being, our friend.' Amy's voice wobbles.

A flicker of surprise crosses the woman's face, which she quickly controls. She looks like the kind of woman who doesn't like to give too much away.

'Of course she was. I'm sorry. I'm writing a story about what happened to her, along with a colleague who's researching for a podcast. Maybe I could ask you a few questions? Over a coffee, or a drink perhaps? I wouldn't take up much of your time.'

Jules is very smart in her trench coat and shiny Chelsea boots, her hair sleek and perfectly straight. Her eyes are small and deep-set and her gaze is penetrating. Does she know I recognise her from the leisure centre? I'll keep that to myself until I've worked out what she's up to.

'Why now?' Kat asks. 'You're a bit late, aren't you?'

Jules is unfazed by Kat's slightly aggressive tone.

'Haven't you heard?' she says. 'New evidence has come to light.'

Daisy shifts beside me.

'Evidence?' Amy repeats. Kat's eyes harden. My stomach twists. 'What do you mean?'

'Hannah's death may not have been suicide after all. The police think she might have been murdered. That's what I'm hoping you can help me with.'

CHAPTER THIRTEEN

'What the …?' Kat says. She doesn't need to finish the sentence. We're back at the car now, relieved to be away from the oppressive clearing, which in a matter of minutes transformed into a possible murder scene. The journalist insisted on giving Amy her card before driving away fast in a smart silver car as if she couldn't wait to put distance between us as soon as it became clear we weren't going to speak to her.

We get back into Amy's car in silence.

'Can you open the windows?' Daisy asks.

I'm behind her in the back, and I inhale a greedy gulp of air as the window slides down. Amy sits rigid, hands clamped on the steering wheel.

'This is huge. Do we believe her?'

Kat drums her fingers on the back of the front seat.

'My gut feeling is no. But it rather depends on what this new evidence is.'

'Agreed,' I say. 'And you're right, it is huge.' Amy's shoulders are hunched up to her ears. I put my hand on her left shoulder. 'Let's go back, Amy, talk about it at the cottage.' An uncomfortable niggle of doubt about what happened to Hannah is lodged firmly in my chest.

'We all need a stiff gin after that shock,' Daisy says.

The rest of the journey takes place in silence, each of us locked away with our own thoughts, processing this new information. The atmosphere in the car is thick with anxiety.

Back at the house, I pull Kat to one side.

'You don't trust that woman, do you?'

'Was it that obvious?'

'Maybe I picked up on it because I feel the same. Don't you recognise her? She was in the leisure centre café. And she followed us to the car park there.'

'No way. I thought there was something weird about her, the way she was watching Amy and Daisy through the trees.'

'Do you think she knew who we were?'

'How could she?'

'If she's been reading up on what happened, she would have seen us interviewed and quoted in that paper, and we're the right age to be Hannah's peers. It doesn't take a genius to work it out.'

Kat's phone beeps and she looks at a message, frowning.

'Everything OK?' I ask.

'Sure,' she says, sticking the phone back into her pocket. I notice her nails are bitten to the quick. 'That journalist being there is really bugging me.'

Amy sinks into one of the garden chairs and we all join her.

'You look done in, Amy,' Kat says. 'What a shock.'

She's right. I decide not to tell Amy about seeing the journalist yesterday.

'I wasn't going to bring this up until later,' Amy says, 'but since we met that woman, everything feels different. It's partly why I wasn't that enthusiastic about the podcast.' She breathes in as if gathering strength. 'I'm wondering if you're all having the same thoughts as me. The thing is, I've always doubted whether Hannah really did kill herself.'

Her words land like hot coals on naked skin. Daisy looks incredulous, and Kat picks at her fingers, fidgeting. For me, her words register with the suspicions that have always been buried deep inside me.

I had my doubts when I first heard about Hannah's death, but I talked it through with my mother and she convinced me it was denial – a coping mechanism – not wanting to believe that my best friend had died by suicide. Hannah's death is by far the worst thing that's ever happened to me: the sense of desperation I felt at not seeing the signs, not being able to stop her, being not a good enough friend. Seeing the way it tore her family apart. So much so that I went to see them less and less, finding each time more difficult than the last, unable to bear the ravages taking their toll on Hannah's mother – the jutting cheekbones and sunken eyes – her father's jolly persona a thing of the past, eventually stopping contact altogether. Which kicked off another cycle of self-recrimination. And on it went.

'What makes you say that?' I ask. The tea in my hand is too hot to drink, and I blow on it, drawing comfort from the warmth. Kat takes another biscuit. It's unlike her; she's normally such a health freak.

'I don't think it's something she would have done. She wasn't suicidal.'

I touch my throat instinctively. Hannah hanged herself from a tree. The rope snapped and she fell and landed in the undergrowth, and a bad thunderstorm thrown into the mix meant her body lay undiscovered for several days. This sequence of events has played over in my dreams ever since. I wake up in a sweat every time. My knuckles are white where I'm gripping the cup, wishing I could unsee the image.

'Take Hannah as a person out of the equation,' Daisy says, 'and think about the police evidence. Nobody else was near that clearing at the time Hannah was there. They have ways of testing, forensic evidence, all that stuff. If the snapped rope hadn't been found, it would have been a verdict of accidental death.'

'There's no CCTV in the car park or anywhere near the woods,' Amy says. 'I wish I'd spoken to that journalist now.'

'Why would you want to do that?' I think of the card the journalist gave her. Maybe Amy's right. Maybe talking to the woman would help. I want to know what happened, after all. But do the others?

'It would be good to know what this new evidence is.'

'It's most likely some guy in prison who's decided to confess,' Daisy says. 'Something like that. What I mean is, it won't have anything to do with us. I don't see any point in upsetting yourself, Amy. It's your birthday today. This could spoil everything. We should never have gone to the forest. I knew it would be bad luck.'

'You didn't have to come,' I say. Daisy gives me a look. 'OK, you did. We made it difficult for you to pull out. But let's not allow this woman to ruin the day. I'm glad we went, despite everything.'

'What about the flowers that were already there?' Amy asks. 'Do you think she left them?'

'Yes, she said she did.'

'Oh. I'd assumed it was one of Hannah's relatives.'

'Are you still in touch with them?'

She shakes her head. 'My mother sends a Christmas card, but that's about it. I should have made more effort. It was too hard. It makes me feel bad.'

'Me too, if it's any consolation.'

Amy gives me a rueful smile.

Kat takes her phone out and looks at the screen.

'I'm going for a walk,' she says, 'I need to make a couple of calls.'

'Theo should be here soon,' I say. 'Have you heard any more from Sam?'

'No,' Daisy says. 'He'd better turn up. I'm going upstairs to give my parents a ring, see how my little brats are behaving. But seriously, Amy, don't let this spoil this evening.'

The teapot is still warm and I pour us both another cup. Amy slumps in her chair and I'm aware how much more relaxed I am when it's just the two of us. The feeling of having to be on my best behaviour around Daisy lifted when she left the room, and Kat is putting me on edge because there is clearly something bothering her. Amy's skin has lost some colour and the tiny lines around her eyes are more visible.

'You really don't think it was suicide, do you?' I say.

'I've always had my doubts. But at the time it seemed like too big a thing to say, when her family were going through such a horrendous ordeal. Do you remember all that stuff that came out in the local paper about her stepbrother having a criminal record? It was ridiculous; he was barely an adult and had nicked a car and gone joyriding with his mates, but they made such a fuss about it. I couldn't believe it. And nobody else had said anything, and …' She sighs. 'We were only young, weren't we, finals were just around the corner, which was bad enough, and it felt like too much of a responsibility to make a statement. The trouble is, right before she died, Hannah told me she'd argued with someone and things would never be the same again. She wasn't the saint you seem to think she is. Maybe it really was murder. Gosh, I can't believe I'm actually using that word.' She lapses into silence, stirring her tea, which doesn't need stirring and is almost cold. 'Do you think Kat is all right?'

The change of subject takes me by surprise.

'Kat? I'm not sure. She seemed pretty shaken by the journalist.'

A jangling sound disturbs our conversation.

'That's the doorbell. I'll go,' Amy says.

I'm lost in thought when strong arms hug me from behind and I inhale Theo's familiar aftershave. I jump up in delight. A flurry of emotions passes through me. He's being affectionate. He's only doing it because Amy's here. Or have we passed another milestone? Whatever it is, I hug him back. He drops his bag to the floor and something clinks.

'You're here.'

'Hello,' he says, and kisses me. *Like he used to.* I hug him hard, wanting to hang on to this feeling of delight at the sight of him, which is usually closely followed by doubts and recriminations. Breathe. *This will work. We will work.* He sits down next to me at the table.

'Want something to drink?' Amy asks.

'A glass of water would be good, thanks, Amy. And happy birthday.' He smiles his lopsided grin and my stomach swoops. With his floppy fair hair and gorgeous smile, I'm still flooded with feelings at the sight of him. Despite everything, this strong physical attraction between us is what makes me believe we have a future. And he wants to have a baby with me.

To think we've come so far since I confronted him with proof of his affair. To his credit, he didn't try to deny it. I offered him a juice and handed him the Post-it note along with it, the bright-pink blatancy of it making me want to heave.

'How long has it been going on?' I said. The tears had been wiped and my demeanour was steely, impenetrable. I wanted to look as if I was the one in charge. He didn't need to know my insides had turned to jelly.

He stared at the note for what felt like forever. His shoulders stiffened and I wanted to yell and shout, but instead I fixed him with a stare. His face looked drained despite his tan.

'I can explain,' he said.

'I'm waiting.'

'Seven months,' he said, 'but it's over now, I swear. It should never have happened. I ended it because I couldn't bear what I was doing to you.'

I wait.

'It happened when we were going through that bad patch, when we were arguing about having children. It felt like a rejection. I was feeling sorry for myself, and she was just there, available. I knew she liked me, she'd made that clear. It was like a drug for a bit, I couldn't get enough, and then she became more demanding and I realised I didn't want her, I wanted you.'

'Were you going to tell me?'

I couldn't get enough. It was like a drug. I wished I'd never heard those words.

He brushed his hair from his forehead, where beads of sweat glistened.

'Yes, no … I don't know. I didn't want to lose you. I *don't* want to lose you. I hate the thought of hurting you.'

'But you did, you have.' My lip was trembling and I bit into it hard, determined not to give in to the tsunami of emotion threatening to engulf me. 'Who is she?'

'You don't know her. She's from work, I met her on that weekend course I did.'

'So she's a personal trainer too?'

'Yes.'

Great. No doubt she was fit and toned and gorgeous, with glowing skin, and I was glad he was sweating and squirming as I stood over him. I was clutching at whatever power I could get.

'I want you to go.'

'Go? Where? You can't … This is my flat too.'

'Just leave, Theo, give me that at least. Go and stay with your brother or something. I need some time to think.'

'So it's not permanent?'

'I don't know. Just give me some space.'

I didn't know anything any more. When he had left, the flat felt empty, vibrating with the words that couldn't be unsaid, words that were forever imprinted in my mind. *I couldn't get enough. It was like a drug.* I gave in to the wobbling lip, and when I'd cried myself out, I fell asleep on the sofa. Only that morning I'd woken with a sense of purpose, a knowledge of a path I was navigating. Now I was a rudderless ship, drifting.

'Have you ladies been having fun?' Theo asks as Amy hands him a glass of water laden with ice. 'It's a great place you've got here, Amy.'

'We have,' she says, and I'm grateful to him for arriving at exactly the right moment, just when Amy needed rescuing from her declining mood.

'We've had pizzas, a climbing wall, a delicious meal – oh, and a steam room,' I tell him.

'And I had a massage,' Amy says. 'Daisy's treat.' She stretches out on the sunlounger.

Theo sets his drink down. 'Is Daisy here?'

'Yes, she's in her room, and Kat's gone for a walk. You've met Kat, haven't you?'

'I have,' he says, 'and Jade. Is she coming too? I'm hoping I won't be the only outsider.'

I give him a playful punch. 'You're not an outsider.'

He grins. 'You know what I mean. Not one of the old gang. Is it weird all being together again?'

'Not at all,' Amy says. She's right: we've slipped into our old dynamic like putting on a familiar coat. 'And we don't know about Jade yet.'

'What's in the bag?' I ask, poking it with my foot. It looks full for Theo, who normally travels light – I'm always amazed when we go away at how little he manages to take with him.

'It's a little surprise for you all. I'm making cocktails later; I'm going to be your personal bartender. I have spirits, fruit, and my very own recipes. And of course the birthday girl will get first-class waiter service.'

'Thanks, Theo,' Amy says, grinning. 'That sounds great. Do you take requests?'

'I do, ingredients permitting.'

'He used to be a bartender,' I say.

'Do you do those fancy tricks, juggling bottles and all that jazz?'

He laughs. 'A little. I'm more interested in the flavours.'

'Fabulous.'

'That's so nice of you,' I say, putting my arm around his shoulder and pulling him in for a kiss. He kisses me back and my body responds; if Amy wasn't with us I'd have dragged him upstairs. *We've still got it.* Reluctantly I pull away, squeezing his hand.

'Have you eaten?' I ask. Theo has a huge appetite and is always hungry.

'I haven't, actually. I didn't fancy anything the train was offering. Any chance of a morsel of something?'

'I can make you a sandwich,' Amy says.

'No, I'll do it. Come on.' I pull Theo up.

'I'll grab a shower then. I'll move my stuff out of the bedroom too, make room for yours.'

Amy goes upstairs and I fill Theo in on what's been happening, leaving out the part about the journalist. In the early days of our relationship, when we were eagerly uncovering each other's lives, I decided he had no need to know Hannah's story – it happened a long time ago and had no bearing on the present.

He nods his head as I talk, one hand pressing buttons on his phone while he devours a cheese sandwich.

'Are you listening?' I ask, experiencing a flash of irritation, the earlier lust forgotten.

'Of course. Oh, hello.'

I follow his look and see Daisy in the doorway. She's changed her clothes and is wearing skinny jeans and a pastel-blue top. She's redone her make-up and looks more like the Daisy we know than the casually dressed version from this morning.

'Hi,' she says.

'You remember Theo,' I say, wishing I didn't have to remind her of that excruciatingly uncomfortable evening we spent together. I haven't had a chance to update Theo on our conversation about it.

'Of course,' she says. 'How was the journey?'

Theo swallows the last of his sandwich and brushes imaginary crumbs from his lips.

He nods. 'Good. How's Sam?'

A dark expression crosses her face. 'He's OK.' She hovers by the table as if she can't decide what to do with herself. 'He's not here yet. I'm expecting an update from him. How are you?'

'I'm fine, thanks.' Theo is stiff and awkward. I didn't expect that evening to have affected him as it did me. It must be in solidarity with me. I feel a rush of affection for him.

'Lou, do you mind if I grab a quick shower?' he says. 'I'm a bit grubby from the journey.'

'Sure. I'll show you where everything is.'

'Cheers. Catch you in a bit, Daisy.'

'OK.' Her phone bursts into an electronic ringtone. 'At last.' She snatches it up. 'Sam, where are you?'

When I've shown Theo where we're sleeping and packed him off into the shower, I go back downstairs. Daisy is in the kitchen with Amy. They both look startled to see me, as if I've disturbed something.

'What's up?' Daisy's posture is rigid and Amy is twisting a curl around her finger.

'You tell her,' Daisy says.

'It's Sam,' Amy says. 'He's going to be arriving much later than he said.'

'That's OK,' I say. 'We already knew that, and it doesn't really matter—'

'No, it isn't OK.' Daisy's sharp tone takes me by surprise, makes me flinch.

'Sorry.' I hold up my hands. 'Nothing to do with me.'

'It's not that,' Amy says. 'It's the reason he's late. He isn't working, like he said he was.'

'I don't understand.'

'He's at the police station.'

'Oh no.' I sit down with a bump on the hard wooden chair. Images of police cars, ambulances, a broken body flash into my mind. 'Has he had an accident?'

'He's been called in to answer some questions.' Amy looks at me as she says this, and a chill envelops my body. I know what she's going to say. Hannah. The journalist. Blackwood Forest. My mind is on fast-forward, willing her to spit it out. 'About what he was doing the day Hannah disappeared.'

Blackwood Independent, 30 April 2005

A witness has come forward in the investigation into the whereabouts of university student Hannah Robinson, missing now for five days. The student was last seen leaving the campus arts building after an English lecture. Friends say Hannah was quieter than normal, but not enough to cause them undue concern. A member of the public, not connected to the university, has reported seeing a girl fitting Hannah's description walking alongside a van along the Blackwood road. Anyone with any further information is asked to contact Blackwood police station.

CHAPTER FOURTEEN

'Apparently they've uncovered some new evidence,' Daisy says.

'It looks like the journalist was telling the truth,' Amy adds. 'She'd obviously heard something and was following the lead for her story.'

'Hannah's not a story,' I say.

'Of course she isn't. That's not what I meant.'

'I didn't mean to snap, it's just—'

'It's fine. It's a shock for us all.'

'What about Sam? What else did he say? Is he still coming here tonight?'

Daisy is running her finger along the grooves in the table.

'He's coming straight after he's finished at the police station. I don't know what exactly they're asking him, or what the evidence is. How *can* there be new evidence? It could just be a ploy to catch him out.'

'That doesn't make sense, Daisy. What would they be trying to catch him out about? They must be interviewing him for a reason.'

'The police always thought the worst of him,' Daisy says, a glint of anger in her eyes.

'He was her ex-boyfriend,' I say. 'They were bound to scrutinise him. I'm sure he'll be fine. I expect they'll be interviewing all of us again; he just happened to be first.'

'Surely not?' Daisy sighs. 'Sam said we should never have come here. Said we were tempting fate.'

'That's nonsense,' I say. 'It's Amy's birthday, Daisy. Let's try and not get too worked up about this.'

'You're right. Sorry, Amy. Sam talks a lot of nonsense. He's got a job on for a very important client at the moment – so important he won't even tell me who it is. He's very stressed, and this is just the last straw. Plus it will make him even later, which means I'll be so wound up by the time he gets here ...'

'So don't be,' I say. 'It's unfortunate – bad timing, whatever you want to call it – but it's out of his control.'

'Yes,' Amy says. 'He'll get here when he gets here.'

'You never change, Amy,' Daisy says. 'You sounded like my mum when you were eighteen, and you're doing a good impression of her now.'

'Someone's got to keep you lot in order. I'm actually pleased, you know, that this is happening. I'm glad that journalist gave me her card.'

'What good will talking to her do? Newspapers tell lies, everyone knows that.'

Amy laughs. 'It's the *Blackwood Independent*, Daisy; it's hardly one of the nationals. Interesting stories don't come around all that often – most local journalists would jump at the chance to cover something other than the opening of a village fete.'

'That woman in her smart coat is intent on going places, that's for sure,' I say. 'I don't think we should get involved.'

'I don't know. She might be able to tell us something. Ever since I told you earlier how I felt about Hannah supposedly killing herself, I haven't been able to get it out of my mind. I'm convinced I'm right.' Amy wrings her hands as she's talking.

'What makes you so sure?' I ask. 'Is it because of the argument Hannah mentioned?'

'Yes, but it was also the texts she was getting.'

'What texts?' Amy's words make me sit up and take notice.

'She told me she was being pestered by someone via text message.'

'Pestered in what way?'

'Unwanted attention, I think. Someone who was interested in her and she wasn't interested in them. She was quite cryptic about it. As if she felt guilty thinking badly about someone. You know what she was like.'

'Yes. A good person. Too good to die.' My eyes fill with tears. Hannah was my best friend. First the depression, now this. Why didn't she tell me about it? I would have done anything for her if I'd had even a hint that she was suicidal. Did I question it at the time? Yes, but she wasn't the sort of person who'd find it easy to seek help; she internalised her unhappiness, and the split with Sam appeared to have sent her over the edge. But suicidal? With hindsight, I'm coming round to Amy's point of view; I don't believe she was. But how well did I really know her?

'Can we please stop talking about this?' Daisy's tone is harsh. 'You all seem to think it's no big deal, but I'm worried about Sam. It can't be very nice for him, can it? He's already said he isn't entirely comfortable coming up here. Hannah had been his girlfriend, and her death devastated him.'

'You're right,' I say, noticing the flush in Daisy's cheeks, her pinched expression. She doesn't find it easy to talk about the fact that Sam was Hannah's boyfriend. 'We're not helping anyone with all this speculation. Let's wait for Sam to get here and tell us what's what – though only if he wants to talk about it, of course.'

'Thanks,' Daisy says, flashing me a grateful smile. 'I'm going to go up to my room for a bit.' She heaves herself out of the chair as if it's an effort to lift her body weight.

The phone in the hall rings as she leaves the room.

'I'll get it,' she says.

'I don't know who that can be. I haven't given this number to anyone,' Amy says. 'I suppose it could be a call for my aunt.'

The murmur of Daisy's voice can be heard from the hall.

'Don't ring here again,' she says, hanging up. Amy and I exchange worried glances.

'Who was it, Daisy?' Amy calls.

She pops her head back around the door. 'It was that journalist woman. How did she know your number? I told her where to go. It's beginning to feel as if we're being persecuted.'

'Slight exaggeration,' Amy says when Daisy has finally gone upstairs. 'I wish I'd answered it. Talking to her might help. If there's even the slightest chance I'm right about Hannah, I will do whatever it takes to uncover the truth about what happened to her.'

'You mean if it's murder,' I say.

Amy looks stunned, as the implication of what this means has finally struck her. She nods her head in slow motion. 'It sounds awful when you say it aloud like that.' She breathes out, to calm herself. 'Has it ever occurred to you?'

'It was my first thought at the time, when we found out she'd died. You know what a private person she was, how hard it was for her to reach out. Obviously Daisy doesn't want us to go there because it has huge implications for Sam.'

'And for all of us. We were the closest people to her. There were all sorts of undercurrents at the time; none of us had straightforward feelings for her.' Amy looks away from me when she says this, and plucks at the leg of her trousers.

'What is it?' I ask.

She gets up and closes the door.

'I have to get this off my chest. Please don't say anything to the others.'

'Of course. You don't need to ask.'

'Obviously this weekend is about Hannah, but my reasons are selfish too.' She breathes in as if drawing courage. 'I've never told anyone this before, but I was jealous of Hannah.'

'Why?'

'Because she had everything. She was clever and beautiful — she had her life sorted. She always got good grades without even trying, while I had to work so hard if I wanted to do well, and I was always terrified of failing my exams.'

As was Hannah, but that was best kept to myself. Her twisted face flashes into my mind, and I push it away.

'Really? You hid it well.'

'I wasn't proud of it. It wasn't how I wanted others to see me. I was jealous of her and Sam too, how she knew what she wanted and had her life mapped out while I bumbled from one day to the next. Having to look after Mum meant I couldn't plan anything, and I resented her for it. I hated myself for feeling like that.'

'We can't help our feelings.'

'Doesn't make them any easier. The thing is, when she split with Sam, my first reaction was satisfaction that at last something wasn't going right for her.' Tears fill her eyes. 'Can you believe that? And then I met Joe and she went to pieces. When we heard she'd died by suicide, I was inconsolable. I couldn't look any of you in the eye; that's why I hid myself away.'

'Oh, Amy. You had nothing to do with her unhappiness, I'm sure.'

'It's not just that. I've felt for ages that someone else was involved in her death, and now, with this podcast and the new evidence, it seems I was right. We all knew Hannah better than anyone.'

'I'm beginning to wonder whether I knew her at all.'

'If anyone else was involved in her death, it could have been one of us. And we have a responsibility to Hannah to find out who.'

'Oh God,' I say, shaking my head. 'I don't want you to be right, but it makes sense.'

My pulse is racing. What if she suspects me? She can't possibly know more than she let on about the argument, can she? I rub my sweaty palms on my thighs as discreetly as possible.

'Don't say anything to the others. It's important that Sam comes, and I don't want Daisy to put him off.'

'Of course.' Sam's more of a suspect than me, surely.

She glances at the clock. 'It's five now. I've got a lot to do. I thought we could start around six, with cocktails. It's so sweet of Theo to do that.' I'm pretty chuffed with him myself, even though it's typical Theo perfectionism. If he's invited to a party, then he has to make it the best party. Acknowledging his good points is a strategy the marriage therapist encouraged me to use, instead of ... I stop there. That's how this works, my mind like a magnet drawn back to the darker times. The pink note, the betrayal ...

'Sure. Six it is. Do you know what you're wearing?'

'It's only us. I'm sure I'll find something appropriate to throw on.'

'Of course you will. Right, I'm going to check on Theo.'

I go upstairs and stop on the landing. Daisy's door isn't completely closed. I knock and stick my head around it. She's sitting on her bed looking at her phone.

'Are you all right?'

She nods. 'Come in.'

I sit next to her on the bed. 'It's all a bit weird, isn't it? I'm finding it harder than I realised, being here, all this emphasis on Hannah. Why is it that I can't remember much about when I was young, yet what happened to her stands out like a flashing police light?'

'It's the same for me, for all of us, I imagine. In a way it's a kind of post-traumatic stress, only that wasn't acknowledged then. It was an out-of-the-ordinary experience. Going over and over it in your mind, wishing you could rewrite your part in it, it's the same for all of us. Especially Sam. This is going to hit him hard, you know. Don't take it out on him, will you?'

'Oh, Daisy, what must you think of me? I would never do that. I like Sam and it will be good to see him. Last time was a blip, and we've been through that. I appreciate it must be hard for him having to go over all this again.'

'I'm worried about him. This is the last thing he needs. He's got so much on at the moment; I had a real job persuading him to come. Don't tell Amy – I don't want anything to spoil this weekend – but I'm even more concerned about her wanting us all to remember Hannah. I'm not sure he'll cope with it.'

'What if you think about it another way? It might be good for him to remember her. I know they'd split up by then, but it still affected him. It can't not have. And being with you would have complicated everything – he wouldn't have wanted you to see how upset he was. Losing someone so young was a first for most of us. Isn't this more about how you're taking it – he might not want you to be upset. If you can reassure him that it doesn't bother you any more, then he'll be less fearful. It might help you to hear his version too – in front of us, I mean.'

She raises her head to look at me. Close up, dark circles line her eyes. 'You just don't get it, Louise. I can never be Hannah. Everyone put her on a pedestal and I can't even get close. She was beautiful and thoughtful and kind, on course for a first-class degree and a glittering future, and everybody loved her. I say what I think, which puts people's backs up, and I do rash things and make mistakes and lose my temper … I can never live up to Sam's expectations, because Hannah always went one better.'

'You think you're not good enough for him? Daisy, that's ridiculous.' Her words have taken me by surprise. It's never occurred to me that she would feel like this. Beautiful, poised Daisy, so apparently sure of herself. Shame I can't tell her that Amy had similar anxieties, but I never break a promise. As she well knows.

'I know you think I'm high and mighty, but it's all an act.' She sighs. 'I'm jealous of Hannah, I admit it. Deep down, I know I can never match up.'

'Nonsense. You're a successful actress, for a start. You and Sam have been married for years and you have two gorgeous children, a whole life together. If Hannah had lived, she would have moved on and what happened would be long forgotten. Like we were saying yesterday, she might even have been here now, Sam an old friend to her and nothing else. It was hard for me at the time, I'll admit, and I let my anger with Sam cloud my judgement for too long, but this weekend is opening my eyes.'

On impulse, I reach for her hand, squeeze it.

'This is a first for us, isn't it? We've never spoken about it before.'

'We should have done this before we went out for that meal.'

I groan. 'You are so right. That was stupid of me. I came with an attitude and Sam picked up on it. It didn't occur to me to put myself in his shoes. And poor Theo didn't know what was going on. I'm glad he and Sam will have a chance to get to know one another this weekend. Talking of Theo, I'd better go and find him. He came up a while ago. I need to make sure he's ready for cocktail hour.'

'Cocktails?' Daisy looks up.

'It was Theo's idea. He's brought some stuff with him. Amy wants us to come downstairs at six.'

'I'm still surprised you invited him.'

'Why? Amy wanted partners to come.'

'He'll be the only one who wasn't at uni with us.'

'Jade's coming.'

'But is she? Maybe Kat's acting weird about it because she's worried Jade will feel awkward about fitting in.'

'I don't think that's the reason.'

I leave her sitting on the bed. Our conversation has made me feel better, but it doesn't look as if it's had the same effect on her. I had no idea she felt inferior to Hannah. Is everybody faking confidence? Those women I admire who step out in front of an audience and give lectures and presentations as if they were born to it, those women at parties who laugh and flirt and work the room, leaving a spill of sparkle in their wake; they all appear to have a confidence gene that is missing from my DNA. I'd always assumed Daisy was one of them, and I'm glad we're getting the chance to get to know one another better.

I stop on the landing and look out over the garden. Kat is coming back towards the house, shoulders slumped. Now there's another confident woman who looks like she's having a hard time. I wonder what she's so upset about.

CHAPTER FIFTEEN

Theo is lying with his arms behind his head, eyes closed. I jump onto the bed next to him. The frame creaks and he opens his eyes, startled, as if he's unsure where he is, one foot in a dream. His expression softens – he's pleased to see me. I still have to check. I think back to not that long ago, when we spent a week apart to make the final decision on our relationship.

I passed the week in a state of agitation, hyper-efficient at work, putting in long hours to avoid making a decision that would affect the way my life would go. I was at a crossroads. The thinking happened mostly at night, when I lay awake feeling lost in my big empty bed, Theo's side cold to the touch. On Friday night, fixating on a crack in the ceiling, the answer came to me that what I had to do was fix this. But would Theo come to the same decision? It was a definitive moment.

He phoned first thing on Saturday, exactly seven days after he'd moved out.

'I have to know what you've decided. I can't wait any longer. Can I come over?'

My heart skipped a beat and I tried to discern his mood from his tone. Upbeat, surely? Or was that an edge of irritation? *Breathe in, breathe out, relax. I'm the one in charge here.*

'Sure,' I said. 'When?'

'Now?'

'Give me an hour. Come at ten.'

To stop myself analysing his words ad infinitum, I rolled up my sleeves and got out the hoover. The flat needed a good going-over. If it was to be bad news, I was going down in style.

As soon as I opened the door, I knew it wasn't bad news. He had hope in his eyes and a large bunch of roses in his hands.

'Flowers don't excuse what I've done,' he said, 'but I want you to have these.'

I fussed around with them in the sink, busying my hands, not wanting him to see the light tremble. Had I read him correctly? Would his decision match mine? I made some coffee and we sat on the sofa. The balcony door was open and the sun poured in.

'How was your week?' he asked.

'OK. Yours?'

'Not good.' He ran his hand through his hair. 'I've spent the whole week kicking myself for hurting you and working out how I can make it up to you. If you want me back, that is. I'll understand if you don't.'

'That's what you want, then? To make a go of it?'

He nodded, hope all over his face. 'What about you? What do you want?'

The week's deliberations flashed through my mind. My decision hovered, giving me one last chance to bat it away, but I'd made up my mind and there was no going back.

'The same. I want us to have a second chance.'

We talked for hours, tentative at first, then braver, trusting one another enough to state our needs. Almost losing one another had made us determined. Marriage guidance counselling would make us stronger, we both agreed on that. By the end of the afternoon we were lying upstairs, my head snuggled under Theo's arm, talking about starting a family. He'd come round to the idea that it was right for us, and I felt complete.

Amy is making a lot of noise in the kitchen, bringing me back to the present.

'Had a nap?' I ask.

Theo puts his arm around me and I snuggle into him. He smells of apple shampoo. Relaxing together feels new, promising.

'What have you been up to?' he asks.

'I got chatting to Daisy.'

'Oh,' he says, pulling a face.

'Don't be like that. We've talked about what happened that night we went out. I apologised.'

'*You* apologised?' He tenses his body.

I prop myself up on my elbow so I can see his face: the dark eyes, the naturally long lashes teenage girls spend hours trying to create for themselves.

'I was in a mood that night – we'd argued about wanting kids right before we went out and I took it out on them. Daisy's got what I want, simple as that. I'm not proud of it.' For a moment I consider telling him the other truth I hold deep inside, but I can't, I promised, and I always keep my promises. 'I should have told you more about our history. Me and Daisy, it's not always been easy. The thing is …' I hesitate, then let the words spill out quickly so I can't unsay them. 'I've never told you about our university friend Hannah. She killed herself.'

'That's awful.'

'She was Sam's girlfriend at the time. Well, just before she died, he left her for Daisy. It was a very difficult time for them both, for all of us.'

Theo looks away from me towards the open window, the pale green curtains blowing in the breeze, the kind of curtains my nan used to have.

'Hannah was my best friend and it took me a long time to forgive Daisy. The six of us were a tight group at university and Hannah's death blew us apart. This weekend isn't just about Amy's birthday. She wanted to get us all back together to commemorate Hannah. To do that, we need to sort out our differences.' Should I tell him about the journalist, the police questioning Sam? I decide against it. At least now he knows about Hannah, and I wouldn't know where to start with the rest of it.

'Are you trying to tell me you don't want me here?'

I sit up. 'No, of course not.' Funny how Daisy mentioned the same thing. 'Of course I want you here. It will help keep us all sane. I want you to like Daisy and Sam. It's important to me. I'm making an effort with Daisy and I don't want to give her any excuse to mistrust me. If you're nice to her too, it will help.'

'Stop worrying. I can play nice with Daisy.'

He pulls me in for a kiss, and I respond but then pull away.

'Don't distract me.'

'I guess we'll have plenty of time for that on Monday.' I look questioningly at him. 'You suggested that an extra day together on our own would do us good. It's a great idea and I took you up on it. I've booked us into a luxury hotel for Sunday night – it's not too far from here. You'll like it.'

Hope surges in me, and this time we linger over the kiss until my watch alerts me that it's half past five.

'Amy wants us down for drinks at six, and we need to get ready. Thanks for the cocktails, that's a lovely touch.'

Just before six, Amy knocks on our door.

'If you want to go down now to prepare, you can. I've finished in the lounge.'

I head downstairs with Theo to help him set up his bar area. I've changed into a black dress and Theo is wearing a suit. Not a stuffy, office kind of suit, but a more casual-looking one, with a long-sleeved crew-neck T-shirt underneath. He looks gorgeous.

'Wow,' he says, coming to a halt in the lounge doorway, making me bump into him. 'I take it this is Hannah?'

Amy has put a framed photo of Hannah in the centre of the mantelpiece. I pick it up with a quick intake of breath. She used to have this photo in her room. It was one Amy took of her on campus, standing in front of the sports centre, laughing, her hair blowing in the wind. Tea lights are placed around it.

Hannah's eyes look at me and it gives me a weird sensation inside.

'I'm not sure I should be here,' Theo says. 'I didn't even know her.'

'You're fine, don't be daft. I want you here.'

Theo goes through to the kitchen while I take in the scene. It feels over the top. This is meant to be Amy's birthday celebration. Thank goodness Kat organised the present and I ordered a cake.

'Did you pick up the birthday cake?' I ask.

He nods. 'It's at the bottom of my bag. What do you want me to do with it?'

'Let's hide it in the kitchen somewhere.'

Amy clears her throat behind us, and I spin around hoping she hasn't overheard.

'What do you think?' Her eyes shine as she looks around the living room.

'What about Daisy? Isn't the picture a bit much?'

'She'll be fine, leave Daisy to me.'

'It's certainly eye-catching, but this evening is supposed to be about you.'

'And it will be. Indulge me, please. It's like an exorcism, getting this out of my system. It will help us all, I'm sure it will.'

'You're the boss. And you look lovely, by the way.' She's wearing a figure-hugging red-and-white dress and her hair is loose. Hannah looks lovely in her photo too, and I wish I could rid myself of the sense of foreboding I feel about the evening ahead. Despite being amongst my oldest friends, this can't end well, no matter how Amy tries to dress it up.

Amy leaves us to set up the bar. Theo clears a counter and lays out his ingredients while I chop up strawberries, lemons and limes and pick mint leaves from a bunch. He produces a small whiteboard on which he writes a list of the cocktails on offer.

Bloody Amy
Mojito
Manhattan
Cosmopolitan
Strawberry Daiquiri
Virgin Any of the Above

'I can't believe you kept all this from me,' I say as I open packets of nuts and Kettle Chips with exotic flavours and empty them into bowls.

'I wanted to do something nice for you.' He looks straight into my eyes as he says this, and my heart melts at the effort he's making. I kiss him on the cheek.

'It's good you've included a non-alcoholic option. Kat doesn't drink much either.'

'I didn't know that,' Theo says. 'I did it for you. Keeping you healthy is my priority, and this way you've got something nice on offer. By the way, where is Kat? I haven't seen her yet.'

'I'm here,' Kat says, coming into the kitchen.

'Hello,' Theo says. 'How's it going?'

'Good, thanks. This all looks very professional. I didn't know you were a drinks connoisseur.'

'I have many talents you don't know about. What can I get you? Take a look at the menu.'

'Bloody Amy,' she says. 'I like it. I'll have one of those, and make it strong. Although it should be called Bloody Jade.'

'Oh?'

Theo and I exchange a glance.

'Yeah, she's not coming.'

'That's a shame,' he says.

Kat shrugs. 'It is what it is.'

'One Bloody Amy coming up.'

'Who's talking about me?' Amy asks, coming in followed by Daisy. Daisy has changed into a white dress, and her hair is sleek and shiny. The tiredness of earlier has been covered with make-up, and she is glowing. Her perfume smells light, summery.

'You've had a drink named after you.' I show Amy the board.

She laughs. 'Cheers, Theo. This is so cool.'

Theo passes Kat her drink.

'Let me take your orders, ladies.'

'I'll have a margarita,' Amy says.

'What exactly is in the daiquiri?' Daisy asks.

'It's made of the finest rum, and plump strawberries.'

Daisy licks her lips. 'Sounds gorgeous. I'll take one of those.'

'Kat was just telling us Jade can't make it.'

'Oh no,' Daisy says. 'Why not?'

Kat drains her glass and hands it to Theo. 'Any chance of another? And extra vodka, please. No, Jade isn't coming. You might as well know, we've split up.' She almost snatches her drink from Theo, takes a long swig and smacks her lips. 'This is perfect.'

'What's happened, Kat?' I ask.

'I wish I knew. I'm going outside for a smoke.' She heads off through the back door.

'That's such a shame,' Daisy says. 'Hasn't she said anything to you, Lou? I thought you were close.'

'Last time we went for a drink, she seemed fine. They were talking about a summer holiday. I wonder what went wrong.' Was Kat hurting in her own relationship and I didn't see it? I could kick myself for not spotting the signs, for being so preoccupied with my own problems. But were there any signs? Maybe I'm being too harsh on myself.

'Do you think I should go and talk to her?' Amy asks.

'No, leave her,' I say.

Daisy's phone buzzes on the table and she picks it up.

'Sam's outside,' she says. Amy makes a move towards the door, but Daisy steps in front of her. 'I'll go.'

Amy and I exchange a glance.

'I hope he's all right,' she says. 'I'll go and see.' She follows Daisy out.

'Why wouldn't Sam be all right?' Theo asks me.

'Something came up that delayed him. And he's been stressed at work. I hope he's not in a mood too.' Though he will be when he finds out Amy's intentions.

Amy comes back in.

'Everything OK?' I ask.

She nods. 'Daisy's just taking him up to stash his case.'

The back door opens and Kat comes in.

'There you are,' Amy says. 'Give me a hug.' She wraps her arms around Kat, who allows herself to be held, her arms hanging stiffly at her sides. After a minute, she pulls away.

'I'm fine,' she says. 'Forget I ever mentioned Jade. Happy birthday to Amy.' She lifts her empty glass in the air. 'Looks like I need another ... Hey, Sam, I didn't know you'd arrived.'

Sam is wearing a suit jacket over jeans and pointed brogues, a subtly patterned scarf around his neck, his hair slicked back to one side. He stood out at university as one of the better-dressed men. Most students lived in jeans and grubby sweatshirts, but Sam shopped in vintage shops and spent longer in the bathroom than any of us women. He's almost as high-maintenance as Daisy, and I wonder whether they fight over bathroom time, then remember they have two bathrooms and a dressing room each, thanks to Sam's hard graft. Daisy must have seen his potential even then.

Don't be bitchy, I tell myself, recalling her telling me how inadequate she felt compared to Hannah, which I would never have guessed at. I feel inadequate compared to Daisy. I notice Theo watching her, and seeing her gorgeousness through his eyes, I feel a rush of jealousy. *Get a grip*, I tell myself. I've asked him to be nice to her after all.

'Oh my God,' Daisy says, catching sight of the photo of Hannah. 'Seriously? What is that doing there? Don't you think it's a bit much?'

Sam follows her gaze. He stares at the photo, shaking his head.

'She was so young. *We* were so young, and we hadn't a clue. It's OK, Daisy. I get what Amy is trying to do, and I'm cool with it.'

'Who wants a drink?' Theo asks, diverting a possibly awkward moment.

Kat helps him organise more cocktails and tops up her own. I resolve to speak to her alone as soon as I can. Whatever she says, she's hurting, and maybe it's not too late for her and Jade.

Once everyone has a drink, Amy asks Sam what happened.

'I had a call from the police,' he says, 'asking me if I wouldn't mind going down to the station. The officer told me it was nothing to worry about, but I must admit, I went into shock. It was the last thing I expected. They asked me about my van at first; I expect you remember the witness at the time who mentioned seeing Hannah walking past a white van.'

Sam was the only one of us driving back then; he used his uncle's old van, which he'd learned to drive in.

'That's old news,' Daisy says. 'We all knew about the supposed van.'

'That's not all. They told me that my phone was found in Blackwood Forest, near to the spot where Hannah died. A dog uncovered it – the owner handed it in at the police station and an officer who worked the case at the time made the connection.'

'Your phone?' Daisy asks. 'But …'

'My old Nokia. Remember I lost it around that time? The weird thing is that the SIM card wasn't in it, which makes no sense to me. I suppose someone threw it away so they could use the phone. But there's more. They checked the area where the dog had been digging and found Hannah's phone too. I don't want to spoil your birthday, Amy, but you're bound to find out soon enough. They told me that the nature of the investigation has changed, and it's now a murder inquiry.' He wipes his forehead, which is sweating.

Daisy gasps. 'Because of the phone?'

He shrugs. 'They implied there was more they weren't telling me.'

'Do they suspect you?'

'Of course they do. I'm an easy target, aren't I? Me and that bloody van.'

'That's outrageous,' she says.

Amy looks thoughtful. 'So that journalist was telling the truth.'

'What journalist?' Sam asks.

Amy explains the situation to him.

'What were you doing in the forest?' he asks.

'We laid some flowers at the spot where Hannah was found.'

He pulls a face. 'It seems a bit of a coincidence that she was there. Do you think she followed you?'

'No, because the flowers she left were already there,' Amy says.

'She did follow us the day before.' I tell them about seeing her at the leisure centre.

'Why didn't you say anything?' Amy asks.

'I just forgot, and it sounds a bit dramatic.'

'Well, now we know she's reacting to the news that the police are asking questions about Hannah's death. Which means …'

'I told you what it means,' Sam says. 'She didn't kill herself .'

'Oh no,' Daisy says. 'This can't be happening. I don't believe that.'

'I do,' Amy says. 'I told you I had doubts at the time. I couldn't accept that she would kill herself. But when her parents didn't contest the decision, I didn't think it was my place to ask questions. What do you think, Sam?'

A conflicted expression crosses his face, and he sighs. 'I don't agree. I'm afraid I do think she could have done it.' He glances at Daisy. 'When we split up, she said she couldn't live without me. I was worried about her, but I couldn't let her blackmail me into staying.'

'Hannah wasn't capable of blackmail,' Kat says.

'Emotional blackmail. You didn't see the texts she sent me, how desperate she was. I wouldn't have got through it without Daisy.' He flashes her a grateful look.

'This is horrendous,' Daisy says. 'What you're saying is that she was murdered. It's too awful to think about. I can't face this again.'

'You'd better get used to the idea, babe,' Sam says. 'They told me they're going to be questioning everyone. I wouldn't be surprised if they turn up here. Save them running around after us all.'

'Not tonight, surely? I knew this weekend was tempting fate.'

'Daisy! It's Amy's birthday. They won't turn up tonight. Did you tell them we were here this weekend, Sam?'

'No.'

Amy looks crestfallen. I wish Daisy would consider the effect her words are having.

'This is a good thing, right?' I say. 'If Hannah was murdered and the police are looking into it, they might find out who was responsible.'

'Of course it is,' Amy says. 'Although it doesn't feel appropriate to be celebrating now.'

We've gravitated to sitting around the kitchen table, with Kat standing by the counter where Theo was preparing drinks. I'm about to ask her what she thinks when she turns slightly and tops her glass up from the vodka bottle. I wonder how much she's had. She scowls into her glass as if she can see Jade's face in it. I wish Jade was here. She's so good for Kat. Or used to be. I'd better get used to using the past tense.

'Let's put some music on,' Daisy says. 'We won't let this spoil Amy's birthday.'

'Good idea,' Theo says. 'Who wants another drink?'

Daisy and Sam start talking and I pull my chair closer to Amy's. 'You OK?' I ask.

'This is huge, isn't it? It feels like a kick in the stomach. Partying feels wrong somehow.'

'What would Hannah have wanted?'

'To be honest, I have no idea. She wasn't a huge party animal, was she?'

'No, but she was fair and good and cared about people.'

'Was she, though? Sam was talking about emotional blackmail. How well did we really know her?'

'I can't see it myself. But she'd want you to celebrate your health and she'd be grateful to you for always believing in her. For seeing what not all of us were able to see. And it means she wasn't as desperately unhappy as we feared, which is a good thing, right?' I add. 'Somebody else deprived her of her life.'

'And I won't rest until I know who,' Amy says.

Blackwood Independent, 1 May 2005

The body of a young woman was found last night by a dog walker in Blackwood Forest. The body has not yet been identified, but is believed to be that of missing Buckinghamshire university student Hannah Robinson.

CHAPTER SIXTEEN

A shrill sound bursts into the room. The doorbell.

Daisy jumps. 'Bloody hell,' she says. 'Could you make that any louder? Your aunt must have been deaf.'

'I'll get it.' Theo goes into the hall.

'You don't think it's that reporter woman, do you?'

We all listen as he opens the door. 'Oh, hello,' he says, and Kat and I exchange a quizzical glance. Their voices rumble. 'Ah yes, I'm Theo. Come in, Jade.'

'What?' Kat frowns. 'Don't say anything about Hannah,' she hisses, obviously forgetting the framed photograph in the lounge.

Theo walks in, followed by Jade. She's wearing jeans and a white vest top under a leather jacket. The white stands out against her dark skin. Her hair is in cornrows and her lipstick is as red as Amy's. A lemony perfume trails behind her. She looks at Kat and I pick up her nerves, her fists curling and uncurling at her sides. I wonder if she'll sense the weird energy in the room, but her focus is solely on Kat, her jaw tense, her lovely face stiff with tension.

'Hi, Jade,' I say, wanting to make her feel at ease, knowing in my gut that she's good for Kat, a stabilising influence.

'Let me get you a drink,' Theo says.

'Something non-alcoholic, please,' Jade replies.

Amy gives her a hug.

'Happy birthday,' Jade says.

'Thanks.'

'Let's go outside.' Kat leads her out into the garden.

'Awkward,' Daisy says when they're safely out of earshot. 'Kat clearly wasn't expecting her. Something's up – all those furtive phone calls, and making out they've split up. What's Jade doing here if that's the case?'

'I don't think you're being fair,' I say. 'Kat's upset about something. I'm sure she would have told us about it in her own time – if she wanted to.'

I'm thirsty and get up to fetch a glass of water. The window is open and the sound of raised voices trickles in, despite the music playing in the adjacent room. Kat's is the predominant voice, and she sounds emotional. Then the back door opens with a clatter as it knocks against the wall, and Jade comes in, cheeks flushed and mouth set. She keeps her gaze on the floor as she pushes past me into the other room. The rush of air that follows her makes me shiver.

I step outside. Cold air catches me by surprise and I wrap my arms around myself. My heels sink into the soft lawn as I make my way down the garden. A shape hovers in the darkness.

'Kat?' It takes a moment for my eyes to adjust to the inky night. An orange glow in the air is the tip of Kat's cigarette. She's facing away from me and starts when I say her name again. 'What's going on?'

She focuses on the cigarette, drawing from it as if it's oxygen, kicking her boot with jerky movements against the roots of the tree she is standing under.

'You wouldn't understand.'

'Try me.'

Laughter filters out from the house – it sounds more like a party now. What are they finding to laugh about? Is it Theo, attempting to divert their attention? Where is Jade amongst this laughter? I hope somebody is looking after her.

'If you don't talk to us, we have to guess at what's in your crazy head.'

'You don't want to know.'

'But I do. You've been there for me big-time these last few months. I'm not sure what I would have done without you to talk to.'

'You and Theo seem to be doing OK.'

'I think we're getting there. It's hard work, and we had to go through a lot of rough times. That's how it works. You get out what you put in.' I can't believe I'm quoting platitudes at someone whose heart is clearly wounded. 'Jade likes you a lot.'

'I know. That's the problem. She asked me to marry her last week. Took me completely by surprise.'

'But that's wonderful, isn't it?'

'Yes. No.' She drops her cigarette butt and grinds it with her heel. 'I can't do it.'

'But you love her, don't you?'

'Yes, I do, but … I can't commit to marriage.'

'It doesn't make sense, Kat. For years you've been searching for your life partner – we were joking only this morning when we were talking about Amy and online dating how you two have traded places. How many times have we scrolled through those dating apps searching for The One? Is it marriage itself that you don't like the idea of? I'm sure Jade would compromise, give you more time, whatever it is you need. Or go for a civil partnership if that would suit you better.'

'It's not that. I don't understand it myself. What if she's not the right person?'

'You won't know unless you try. Theo isn't the kind of guy I thought I'd end up with. Sometimes you have to break the pattern. Take a risk.'

'When did you know he was a keeper?'

I think back to how unsure I was when Theo first moved in. It was a big commitment, and what if it didn't work out? I'd bought my place a few years before with help from my parents for the deposit; if it wasn't right for us, then he'd have to go. But he settled into my routine like a pair of old slippers, and I let my guard down, admitted to myself I needed someone else and embraced the relationship.

'Quite soon after we started living together. We got on great and had a lot of fun. He made me realise what had been missing from my life before I met him. He helped me to relax, chill out more. I went out less because I didn't need to keep busy to stop myself getting lonely. He made me feel good about myself. We were great ...' *Until he had an affair.*

I stab at the discarded cigarette butt with the pointed toe of my shoe. Kat throws me a sympathetic look; I don't need to elaborate to her. I kick the remains of the cigarette away.

'But we're through that now. No small thanks to you for listening. Which is why I'm here. You've seemed so much happier since you met Jade. I don't want you to throw that away lightly. Maybe you're not ready for marriage yet, but you don't have to go that far if it doesn't feel right. If you're sure it's over between you and it isn't what you want, then of course I've got your back, but ...' I shrug. 'Don't forget we're all under stress this evening; it's not the best frame of mind to be in when you need to make a big decision. Why not try and forget about it until you're back in London?'

Kat stands by the garden wall and looks out across the field towards the forest, where the trees swish in the wind, whispering their secrets into the air.

'She's most likely gone now anyway. The proposal isn't the only problem.'

'What's up?'

She shrugs. 'It's private.'

'You can tell me anything.'

'No, I can't. Leave it, Lou. Talking might help you, but we're different people. I know you mean well, but back off. You're not making this any easier.'

She turns away from me. Her back is like a slap in the face. Music from the house swells into the garden as the back door opens. Jade is silhouetted against the light. I cross the lawn, stumble in the dark. The light picks out the creases in her leather jacket. It looks worn, comfortable.

'Are you OK?' I ask.

'Not really. Has she told you?'

'About the proposal? Yes. She's not making much sense, to be honest. I thought you two were good together. She won't talk to me. There's something she's not telling me, but it's between you two; I get it.'

'You think it's worth another go? My pride is at stake here.'

'Look, we've had quite a heavy weekend. We went through a difficult situation when we were all at university, which we've been reliving this evening, and emotions are running high. Please don't give up on her just yet. I've told her that you're the best thing that's ever happened to her. She'd be mad to let you go.'

Jade throws her arms around me, squeezes me tight. Her leather jacket is cool against my skin.

'Let's hope you're right. You go inside, you look cold. I'm staying out here for a bit.'

'Good luck.' I watch her walk down the garden into the darkness. From where I'm standing, it looks like she's been swallowed up by the forest. I recall my dream, the gnarled roots of the ancient trees tripping me up and winding themselves around my feet. Who lured Hannah into that same forest all those years ago? I can't get into the house quickly enough.

Daisy is sitting on the sofa talking to Theo. She gets up when she sees me and joins the others. I take her place on the sofa.

'What were you two talking about?'

'Hannah. I wish you'd prepared me for this. It's all a bit heavy-duty. And what's up with Kat? She's normally so easy-going. Is her row with Jade mixed up in all this?'

'No, Jade doesn't know anything about Hannah either.'

'I'm glad it's not just me. Why didn't you tell me before now? Did you know that this' – he gestures with his arm around the room – 'this evening was going to be so intense?'

'Not exactly. The photo is Amy's doing. It's a bit weird, to be honest. OTT. But we haven't been together as a group since that time, and it was bound to come up. That's why I was so nervous.'

'I didn't realise you were. Which doesn't help us, does it? We're supposed to be having a fresh start based on trust and being open with one another. That has to mean everything, otherwise it means nothing.'

'Everything has changed since Sam dropped his bombshell. We're talking murder here. I'm glad Amy put that picture up. It means we can't forget. We need to do something, get to the bottom of what really happened to Hannah.'

My voice has risen, and Theo glances around. 'I want to understand,' he says quietly. 'Daisy tells me the reason it's so difficult for you is because you came down really hard on Sam for leaving Hannah.'

Blood rushes to my head. Why is Daisy telling Theo this? Is she trying to cause trouble between us? I look around to check where she is – the last thing I want is her hearing this conversation – but she's over with Amy, leaning against the wall and laughing at something.

'Is that why you've been so tough on me?' he asks.

'We've been through all this with the counsellor. We agreed it doesn't help to go over it again.'

'We did, but you've been acting funny with me.'

'No I haven't.'

'You have. You don't trust me. It's like there's a barrier between us, and I'm scared of getting too close.'

'That's not true. We've been planning our future, a move away from London. That's huge for me. Agreeing to have children is a massive deal, but now we've talked about it as a real possibility, I can't wait. I want to have children with you. That's why I'm not drinking this evening.'

'That's what I wanted too.'

The change of tense makes my stomach clench.

'Wanted?'

'All this tonight, this Hannah business. How do you think I feel not knowing anything about an event that has clearly had a massive influence on your life? It makes me wonder what else you haven't told me. I'm an open book for you. All that stuff I told you about my childhood, what it was like growing up with a single dad who preferred alcohol to me. It wasn't easy sharing all that. It makes me think you don't value me enough.'

'I don't get why you're saying this.'

'Because of what Daisy told me. She said you have very high standards when it comes to relationships, and you've never forgiven her, or Sam, despite what you say.'

'High standards?' If wanting someone I get on well with and fancy to death and who makes me feel good about myself is high standards, then I'm guilty, but otherwise it's just not true. It makes it sound as if Theo isn't good enough for me. I glance over at Daisy. She's his type: petite and curvy, blonde hair. I was going through a blonde period when I first met him. She oozes sensuality just in the way she's leaning against the wall. I'm transported back to student days. She used to flirt with everyone, and I wasn't the only woman she made feel insecure. But she's got Sam now; what would be the point?

'I don't believe this,' I say. 'I've made a real effort with Daisy this weekend. I thought we were making progress with our friendship.

Getting back to how we used to be. Think about it, Theo. Why is she telling you all this when you barely know her? She's trying to cause trouble between us. I've seen the way she looked you up and down when you came in, measuring you up. She can't bear for me to be happy.'

'Rubbish,' he says. 'We were just making conversation. She asked me if you and I talked about Hannah much. I had to fess up that I had no idea about any of this. I felt about this big.' He indicates an inch with his fingers. 'We talked about the new police investigation. How do you feel about that?'

'We're all still in shock, I think, but it's a good thing.'

'Will people be able to remember what happened? It was a long time ago.'

'Everything about that time is clear to me. It's like the day my gran died; some things you never forget. I've been over this so many times it even enters my dreams. But I never find the answer I'm looking for.'

'I'm the same. I'll never forget the day my mum left.'

I take his hand instinctively. 'That's what I mean. It's one of *those* moments. I'm glad you understand. I want you to know about Hannah too. I promise I'll tell you everything. She's important to me, to all of us.'

He squeezes my hand and I love him for getting straight on my side.

'Don't be too hard on Daisy,' he says. 'We've all had a few drinks. Everyone is tense.'

CHAPTER SEVENTEEN

Theo goes outside for some fresh air. His remark leaves a sting; why is he sticking up for Daisy? Sam is sitting on his own looking through what must be Amy's aunt's vinyl collection. He slides an album out of its sleeve, holding it up to the light from the lamp placed behind him, casting a shadow across his face and picking out his slanted cheekbones, his stubbly chin. His good looks haven't lessened with age. He and Daisy are still a striking couple.

'There's some interesting stuff here,' he says.

'You should ask Amy if you can have some of them. I imagine she'll have to sort through all her aunt's possessions and decide what to do with them. You'd be doing her a favour.'

'Daisy won't be impressed. She's always moaning that I've got too much junk everywhere. She likes everything to be reduced to a minimum.' He picks at the material on the cushion he's sitting on. Close up, I see lines etched into his skin, evidence of the years since we first knew one another. 'She had to force me to come, you know. Last thing I wanted to do was return here, revisit that awful time.'

'Isn't being with Daisy a constant reminder?'

'No, because now that we've got the kids, it's like two separate lives. Young me and adult me. I did some stupid things back then. I wish I'd done things differently with Hannah, but I was just a boy, and I'm not going to spend the rest of my life beating myself up about it.'

'Was it true what you said earlier about Hannah, the emotional blackmail?'

He rubs his face. 'It's not easy saying this – I don't like to speak ill of the dead and all that – but living with Hannah wasn't easy. She was insecure, and could be very jealous, and at times she went too far. She'd lash out at me, try to stop me seeing my friends. Especially female friends. Even you lot; she gave me a hard time about how close we were.'

'Seriously? Why didn't you say something before?'

He gesticulates towards the photo. 'Because you all adored her. It feels disloyal. And I did love her, for a long time.'

He goes back to examining a record sleeve and I sense he wants to be left alone.

Jade is standing by herself in the corner, clutching a glass to her chest. I beckon her over and we move to the sofa, leave Sam to his records.

'Who's she?' She points to Hannah's photo looking down at us.

'She was our friend at university who disappeared. It hit us all hard and we wanted to remember her.'

Jade starts.

'What is it?'

'Nothing. Sounds a bit weird, that's all.'

'I guess it does. For what it's worth, Kat's been in a strange mood all night; she was knocking back the drink earlier and I think it's partly to do with this evening and remembering her.'

'Was she ever found?'

'She was. She killed herself. Or so we thought. The police now think it was murder. They've reopened the case and we've only just found out.'

'That's awful. But this is a perfect example of the way Kat is with me. Why does she never tell me anything?'

'To be fair, I didn't tell Theo about it either. It's complicated. Maybe that's why she didn't want you here.'

'Nice try, but that's not the case. She was really excited about me coming until I made my stupid proposal.'

'It wasn't stupid. How did you get on just now? Have you patched things up?'

'Hardly.' She frowns at the glass she's still clutching. 'But we've talked. At least now I know where I stand.'

I wait, not wanting to push her if she doesn't want to confide in me. I'm Kat's friend after all, although Jade and I clicked the first time we met. The three of us went to a quiz night at Kat's local pub and managed to come last, but had a hoot in the process. When Jade had gone to the bathroom, Kat told me excitedly that she'd found The One. I've seen the way she looks at her. Kat has seemed more at ease in her own skin these past few months, as if she's no longer searching for something to fix herself. I don't want to believe that's over already.

'I should get going. Kat's made it clear we're finished.'

'Oh no. I'm so sorry, Jade.'

'Don't be. At least I know the reason.'

'Can I ask what it is?'

Her eyes brim with tears. 'She said she loves me very much, and it's nothing to do with me, but … she went to great pains to make sure I understood she would *never* be able to commit because she's in love with someone else.'

'No.' That's the last thing I was expecting.

'Not in the way you're thinking. She's still in love with her first love, the love of her life.'

My brain whirs, trying to recall what Kat has told me about her past relationships.

'She's put this person on a pedestal and nobody can ever come close. It's so sad, makes me so angry. Surely that isn't real love?'

'I guess it depends whether that person is still around, and how they feel about her. I presume it's a she?' Kat's comment about Alison Postlethwaite springs into mind. Was there more to it than a crush?

Jade nods, wiping her eyes, which are black with leaking mascara.

'Yes, it's a she. Kat wouldn't tell me who it was, but her mum inadvertently let something slip. I get on really well with her and she told me once that she'd known Kat was gay since she was at university because she used to talk about her girlfriend all the time. Now Kat had already told me she didn't have a relationship with anyone until she was at university, so this girlfriend has to be her first love, right?'

'Yes, right, except Kat didn't date anyone at university. At least as far as I know.' How well do you ever know another person? Amy's words from earlier echo in my head. Maybe Kat has always hidden part of herself away, and I've only become aware of it more recently. At university there were so many other people around, so much going on, so many distractions. It was easy to slip under the radar.

Jade frowns. 'That can't be right. Polly – Kat's mum – said she was crazy about her.'

'Did she tell you anything about her?'

'Yes. Apparently her name was Hannah.'

My mouth drops open.

'Are you OK?' Jade asks.

A craving for a cigarette to settle the queasiness in my stomach consumes me.

'No. I'm in shock. Hannah was the name of our friend who died. Who was murdered. The woman in the photo.'

Jade claps her hand to her mouth.

'But Kat didn't go out with Hannah. She didn't date anyone during the whole three years, until she met Diane, but that didn't last long. None of her relationships have ever lasted, which is why we were all so thrilled about you. You've been so good for her.'

'I don't understand any of this. Why would she say that? Maybe you didn't know? She wouldn't be the first gay person to hide a relationship. It's not always easy to be out.'

'But that doesn't make sense. She came out to us when we first met her; she never made a secret of it.'

'What about Hannah?'

'She was with Sam. They got together in the first term and lasted until shortly before she disappeared.'

'Sam?' She lowers her voice. 'Him with the records?'

'Yes, he left her for Daisy. It was a very difficult time. Hannah wasn't gay.'

'As far as you know.'

'Yeah, obviously it could have been something she kept to herself, or maybe she identified as bisexual. I'm starting to wonder whether I ever knew her at all.'

'No wonder there's such a strange atmosphere. When I walked in, it felt more like a wake than a party, and now I know why.'

'Maybe you should stick with Theo. He's neutral too.'

'But I'm not. Hannah is stopping Kat from loving me. And she's not even alive.' She wipes her face. 'I know what to do now. Kat doesn't know what her mum told me, or that I know it was Hannah. What she needs is help to stop her from being stuck in the past. If I can get her to open up about it, we can work through it together. Do you mind not telling her I know?'

I shake my head. 'You really do love her, don't you?'

She nods. 'I can't stand seeing her hurting like this. I feel it too, you know?'

I feel a pang of loss. Theo and I used to be like that; in the old days if we'd been at a party, even if we weren't physically together in the room, I'd always know where he was as if an invisible string was connecting us, or he'd give me a look and I'd know he'd been thinking about me. We'd strive to find solutions to our problems in the same way Jade is now. This evening that connection is stretched, and I'm not sure we'll ever get it back.

'I've got nothing to lose by telling her what I know. I may have lost her already, but I won't go without a fight.'

'Be careful,' I say, unable to explain the frisson of fear I feel at thinking about Kat and Hannah. What if they really had been having a secret relationship? Or worse, what if Kat had created a full-blown love affair with Hannah in her mind? Exactly how disturbed would she have to be to do that? Everything I thought I knew is tumbling down around me.

Amy's comment about unwanted attention flashes into my mind, and another possibility occurs to me, sending a shiver of fear down my spine. What if Kat was coming on strong to Hannah, adding to her distress over the break-up with Sam? How far would she be prepared to go?

CHAPTER EIGHTEEN

Amy comes over to join us.

'You OK?' I ask.

She nods. What with all the Kat and Jade drama, I've been forgetting Amy. The evening needs a purpose. Now would be a good time to get the cake, focus on her. Kat and Sam are the only other ones in the room.

'Let's get everyone together and play a game or something. Sam, where's Daisy?'

He shrugs. 'Bathroom, maybe? She's been gone a while.'

'I'll go and find her,' Amy says. 'You get Theo.'

She leaves the room and I ask Jade to fetch the cake from the kitchen, pointing out the cardboard box where it's hidden. 'Sam, you choose some music. We're going to get everyone together.'

'About time,' Kat says. 'This is supposed to be a party.'

A full moon shines over the garden and a dog is barking in the distance. Halfway down is a wooden shed that's seen better days, and there's a large tree in the corner by the back fence. The lawn needs cutting and weeds sprout everywhere. I can't see Theo, so he must be somewhere at the end of the garden. I've just reached the shed when I hear his voice and come to a halt, because I recognise the tone he uses when he's annoyed. I catch sight of myself in the shed window; my face is pulled into a frown. Theo doesn't know anyone here well enough to argue with them. He must be on his phone to one of his friends, but I'm failing to convince myself that he'd be half hidden in the darkness behind a shed arguing about politics or something. My gut tells me to hold back, listen some more. Then I hear the soft tones of a female voice.

'I told you not to come.'

It's Daisy.

Her words sound so personal, I slump against the shed and put my hand over my mouth to stop myself from making a noise. My heart is thumping so loudly I'm convinced they will hear it, and I'm desperately trying to convince myself that nothing is wrong, despite the suspicion coursing through my body.

'How could I not? All we had to do was stay away from each other. You've risked everything by following me out here. If you felt so strongly about it, you should have stayed away yourself.'

'Don't be ridiculous. Of course I had to come. Amy is one of my oldest friends. Have you any idea how difficult this is for me, having to be here with Louise and look her in the eye? It's excruciating. It's bad enough that she's never forgiven me for stealing Sam from her precious Hannah.'

'I thought you'd sorted that.'

'I'm not convinced. Are you sure she doesn't know about us?'

'I told you, she has no idea. It's all in your head. You're making it worse by following me out here. I told you to stay away from me, act as if we don't know each other.'

'I had to speak to you. I'm sure Sam suspects something.'

'Oh Christ.'

I can picture exactly how Theo is standing and the expression on his face. His body goes rigid when he's stressed, and he tenses his hands, his fingers curling and uncurling like the tentacles of an octopus. It infuriates me. I need to hang on to those things that infuriate me about him. Do the opposite of the therapist's advice. I might be needing them.

'What are we going to do?'

'There is no *we* any more, Daisy.'

I close my eyes. Do I dare to hope? I'm hanging on to his words and I hate myself for still wanting him.

'Lou doesn't know and I intend it to stay that way. You'll have to deal with Sam. Now go inside before anyone wonders where we are and comes looking for us. Just keep your cool and we'll be fine.'

Daisy and Theo, Theo and Daisy: the words flash in my head and I want to scream. Instead I hold myself still and control my breathing. I have to work out what this means and how to play it. I won't let Daisy – or Theo – get away with what they've done.

My feet are rooted to the spot with shock, and it takes a moment for me to react when I hear them moving. I scurry back across the lawn and slip into the kitchen.

'There you are.' Kat's voice is loud, drunk-sounding. 'You took ages. Did you find him?'

I open my mouth to speak, not sure that any sound will come out, but Daisy steps into the room and Kat turns her attention to her.

'There you are, Daisy – ah, and here's Theo. What's going on out there? This is where the party is at. Ready, everyone? Happy birthday …' she sings loudly and the others join in; I mouth the words, my mind still out in the garden. Jade cuts the cake and passes pieces around. When she gets to me I shake my head. Kat leads a round of applause, then holds up her hand for quiet.

'Come and sit down – I've had a brilliant idea. Come on, Lou, why are you standing there looking like a lemon?'

'I need a drink,' Daisy says to Sam.

'Where've you been?' My voice sounds normal.

'Fresh air.' Daisy flicks her hair back and I can't look at her any more. My legs feel unsteady and I plonk myself down on the nearest chair and take my phone out of my pocket, pretend to be interested in something on the screen, will my body to stop shaking. I need a strategy to handle this.

'No phones,' Kat says. 'I've had a great idea to liven this party up. Let's have a game of truth or dare.'

'We're not at university now,' Daisy says. 'Isn't that a bit childish?'

'Don't be such a bore. Being in your thirties doesn't mean you can't have a bit of fun. It's your party, Amy, you decide. Do you fancy it?'

Amy looks around at the others to gauge their reactions.

'Count me out,' Theo says. 'I'm just the bartender.'

'Coward,' I say.

'I'd have to bail anyway if I was asked to kiss someone else apart from you.' He grins at me.

I force my face to smile back. He makes me want to vomit. My mind is whirring with possibilities of how to use this new knowledge. Deep breathing helps, and so will a drink. A real drink. Fuck juice and folic acid and priming myself for conception. A hard lump lodges in my throat.

'Could you pour me a glass of wine?'

'You sure?'

I look him in the eyes, daring him to defy me.

'I'm very sure. Make it a large one.' I drop my gaze and switch my attention to Kat. 'This game sounds like a great idea. And Theo, you must take part. A few dares won't do you any harm.' *And maybe a few truths might spill out along the way.*

'Of course it's a great idea,' Kat says. 'You want to play, don't you, Amy?'

I'm not sure this is Amy's thing. We used to play card games back in the hall of residence – it became addictive for a while, and a game was always going on around the kitchen table – but truth or dare? It's not really her style.

'Come on, Amy,' Kat says. Her voice is louder each time she speaks. Sam exchanges a glance with Daisy. I'm not sure he signed up for this. There are several truths I'd like to dig up, but there are others I most definitely want to stay buried. And all of those involve Hannah.

'OK, all right.' I'm pretty sure Amy is only saying this to shut Kat up. 'Let's sit in a circle in the living room; it's too cramped in here.'

Everyone moves into the lounge. The room is lit by one lamp, and the tea lights flicker as we move. We form a rough circle, some sitting on the carpet, some on the sofa and chairs.

'Give us a bottle, Theo,' Kat says, 'and I'll do the first spin.'

Theo locates an empty wine bottle and rinses it out before passing it over. Kat drops to her knees and spins the bottle rather too hard; it flies across the floor and hits me in the leg.

'Ouch! Watch out, Kat. Don't give her any more of those cocktails.'

'Ignore her, spoilsport,' Kat says, retrieving the bottle and spinning it again. The neck comes to a halt in front of Amy, who groans.

'I've changed my mind about playing,' she says.

'Too late,' Kat says. 'Truth or dare?'

Amy looks around at our expectant faces, all focused on her.

'Oh, dare, I suppose. You'd better not make it too outrageous, though.'

Kat spins the bottle again to see who gets to set the dare. 'Louise.'

My thoughts are darting like arrows and I force them to focus, relieved it's not Kat I've landed on, not sure I'd dare ask her the truth about Hannah in front of everyone.

'I dare you to message the guy on Bumble you liked the look of and set up a date.'

'Yes!' Daisy says, clapping.

'What's this?' Sam asks.

'We encouraged Amy to sign up to a dating website,' Kat tells him.

'He'll be lucky to have you,' Sam says.

'Go on then,' Kat urges her, 'get your phone.'

'Oh for God's sake.' Amy laughs, pulling her phone from her pocket. 'OK, but he'd better be worth it.' She taps out her message, shows us the screen and hits send. 'Satisfied?' Then she reaches out and spins the bottle. This time it lands pointing at Kat.

'Ha!' Amy says. 'Time to get my own back. Truth or dare?'

'Truth,' Kat says.

Amy spins the bottle again and it stops in front of Daisy. Theo comes in and puts a bottle of wine on the table along with some bowls of crisps, before pulling a chair up to join us. He's closer to Daisy than me.

'OK,' Daisy says. 'My truth question is, what's going on with you and Jade?'

'Daisy,' Amy says, glaring at her. Jade stares at the crisps.

Kat picks at the carpet with her fingers. 'That's easy.' She looks at Jade. 'I don't know.'

'Do you want me to go?' Jade asks.

Kat shakes her head. 'No. In answer to your question, Daisy, let's just say I'm having commitment issues.' She's trying to make light of it. 'Let's carry on with the game. Next.'

As she reaches for the bottle, she loses her balance. Sam grabs her and stops her from toppling over. She spins the bottle and it stops in front of him.

'Truth or dare?' Amy asks.

'Dare,' he says.

'Hang on.' Kat snatches up the bottle. 'I've had a much better idea. Let's forget this dare nonsense; what we all want is the truth.'

'Meaning?' Sam asks.

'Meaning there's one question that has been on everyone's minds since we first got here. What happened to Hannah? Amy's been banging on about wanting to remember her' – Amy flinches at this – 'so why not go round the room and ask each of us the same question?'

'Which is?' Sam asks.

'What happened when you last saw her?'

A stunned silence follows.

'Think about it,' Kat says. 'We've never come together like this and pieced through Hannah's movements those last couple of days. We'd be doing her a favour. Sam's already warned us the police are going to be asking questions, so why not get our stories straight?'

'You make it sound like we've got something to hide,' I say.

'Maybe somebody has. What do you think? I'm just putting it out there.'

Another silence. Are the others going through those moments that are forever imprinted on their memories as clearly as they are on mine? Or have they forgotten the details with the passing of the years? I watch Amy, trying to work out what she makes of all this.

'It's not a bad idea, actually,' she says finally. 'It might jog our memories. It might help us get to the truth.' Her eyes glint with excitement. 'Yes, let's do it. I wanted to remember her, but this way we might be doing her a service as well. Finding her killer.'

'And how do you know the killer isn't in the room?' Theo asks.

'Steady on,' Sam says. 'One interrogation is enough for one night.'

I stare at Theo, amazed. 'What on earth …? You don't know anything about it.'

'True, but I have been listening to you all this evening, and Hannah doesn't sound like the sort of person who attracted enemies, or liked to draw attention to herself. If anyone had reason to kill her, it's likely to be someone close to her – most people are killed by someone they know. I can be objective.'

'I wasn't suggesting that for a minute,' Amy says. Her face looks pale in this light. 'But we might find out a bit more about what really happened in her last few days. What do the rest of you think?'

Daisy looks at Sam. 'Are you all right with that, babe?'

He shrugs. 'I've got nothing to hide.'

'Going back to what Theo said,' Daisy says, 'I disagree that Hannah was as sweet as you all make out. Maybe if everyone answers the question truthfully, the rest of you will come to see that too.'

'This isn't about blackening her character,' I say.

'That's not what I meant. Can you honestly say you never saw a different side to her?' Our eyes meet and I force myself not to look away, telling myself she can't possibly know about our argument. Even if Hannah *had* spoken to someone about it, Daisy was the last person she'd have confided in.

'At least it will get us out of doing any more stupid dares,' Kat says. She's more focused now. Has she only just come up with this idea, or is it a set-up? Maybe she's been planning it all along. But why? My stomach churns.

'Is that a yes, then? We'll go round the circle anticlockwise. Which means, Amy, you're up first. So here it is, the big question. What happened when you last saw Hannah?'

CHAPTER NINETEEN

Amy, Daisy, me, Sam, Kat. That's the order of the game. Jade is between Kat and Amy, but she won't be playing, and Theo is between me and Daisy. I angle myself away from him, needing distance. Amy is in the large armchair, legs folded under her, but when Kat asks her the question, she unfurls her body and sits up straight, looks round at us all. It's as if she's about to open a picture book and read to us. I wonder what story she will tell us, wonder how, when we've all told our stories, the overall picture will be different. Why have we never done this before? Was it fear that stopped us?

'OK. The last time I saw Hannah was the day before she went missing. It was late afternoon, maybe around five, and she knocked at my door. She'd been studying in the library all day and she looked shattered. You have to remember, Hannah was one dedicated student, always had been, but that last term she took it to a whole new level. It was the final term for us, the crucial time before finals, and the pressure was really getting to her. Which surprised me in one way, because although she was a born worrier, she'd worked so hard the whole time she'd been at university.'

'Unlike the rest of us,' Daisy says. 'Everyone I knew did the bare minimum, wrote essays the night before they were due in, which meant last-minute panic every year when exams came round.'

'We all used to take those herbal tablets that were supposed to help you stay up late,' Amy says, 'but not Hannah, she didn't usually need to. But so much in her life had changed. As well as finals looming, her first big relationship had come to an end and she was dealing with that too. So anyway, she stopped by my room and I invited her in to chill out for a bit, but she said she wouldn't because she needed to go and have a sleep but she'd catch me later. We'd developed a routine of her coming in to me for a herbal tea and a natter before she'd go off to bed around midnight. I think she found evenings hard to get through. That evening she came back at about half past nine and said she hadn't been able to sleep. I suggested she make an appointment at the medical centre, because she was really on edge. She said she kept waking up throughout the night and despite being so tired she just couldn't get back to sleep. She was on the waiting list to see the student counsellor, but she said she was OK, because the end was in sight.'

'She said that?' Sam is suddenly paying attention. A moment before, he'd looked like he wasn't even listening. '*The end in sight* sounds pretty ominous to me.'

'Exams, that's what she meant. Soon exams and uni would be over and she could go home.' Amy looks around at the rest of us, horrified. 'You don't think …?'

'No,' Kat says, not sounding totally convinced. She appears to have sobered up rather quickly.

'No' – Amy nods – 'she didn't mean that, because prior to that evening she'd told me that as soon as exams were over, she planned to go home and spend the summer with her family. She was looking forward to it so much – that's why I don't believe she would have killed herself.

'But anyway, back to that evening. She kept checking her phone. I asked her if she was expecting a message, and she said no, but she kept checking it anyway, like a nervous tic. I didn't believe her. Just when she was about to go back to her room – it was pretty late, gone eleven – she received a text and looked really shaken up. I asked her what was going on and she burst into tears and said somebody was harassing her. It transpired that she'd got into a situation with someone who was romantically interested in her and wouldn't take no for an answer. At first she thought she could handle it and tried to be friendly but firm, but this person wouldn't give up. I asked her over and over who it was, but she wouldn't let on; she wanted to protect their identity, which was so typically Hannah. I guessed it must be somebody I knew, otherwise why not tell me?'

Jade and I exchange a glance, and my stomach twists.

'There was that guy in her tutorial group,' Kat says. 'He was a bit weird, and he liked her a lot. We used to tease her about it. She said he'd always manage to sit beside her, and her tutor's room was tiny so it was a bit of a squeeze. What was his name? Mark, maybe?'

'I know who you mean,' I say. 'Mark Gallagher. I doubt it would have been him. He got together with Stella, who was also on our course, and his interest in Hannah vanished overnight. I think he just wanted a girlfriend.' I can't help wondering whether Kat is trying to deflect attention away from herself.

'Poor Stella,' Kat says. 'Typical man.'

'Anyway, she wouldn't tell me, and shortly after that, she went off to bed. I couldn't stop thinking about what she'd told me, and the next day I resolved to try and find out who it was. But I never got the chance. I didn't find out she was missing for a while. I was worried when she didn't turn up the following night as she always did, but I didn't knock at her door in case she was sleeping. It was the day after that that the university police officer came to the halls asking about her, and then … well, you know what happened after that.'

'Did she give you any clue about this admirer at all?' Daisy asks. 'Presumably it was another student? Or it could have been a lecturer? That would have been a difficult situation to navigate, and she might have been too scared to tell anyone about it.'

'That was my first thought, and I went through the staff in my mind. Hannah and I were on exactly the same courses, so I knew who she came into contact with, though she had a different tutor to me. Most of the department were female – of the ones who taught us there were around five women and three men. Nothing untoward ever happened in class as far as I remember. I just can't see it. Hannah was so enthusiastic about her seminars and tutorials; she always looked forward to them. She was unusual in that respect. If she was being put into an awkward situation with a professor, she'd be reluctant to go to class, surely? And like I said, I was always there.'

'Her tutor, then?' Daisy suggests. 'Did you know him?'

'He didn't teach me, but it was Professor Galloway. He was gay, made no attempt to hide it.'

The mention of Professor Galloway is so unexpected, I flinch as if I've been struck. I quickly scan the faces around me, but nobody else appears to react – until I get to Amy. She looks away when our eyes meet, and my heartbeat accelerates. Does she know?

'I knew him,' Kat said. 'He came along to the LGBT Soc meetings sometimes. He was most definitely out and proud. We all looked up to him.'

'Someone on her course, then,' Daisy says.

I shrug. 'I can't imagine who it could have been.'

Amy shakes her head. 'I feel terrible about it because she'd hinted at it a few weeks earlier, and that was when I'd just got together with Joe.'

Daisy squeals. 'Joe! I'd forgotten about him.'

'That's the best thing to do,' Amy says. 'I wish I could.'

'We hardly saw you once he showed up. Talk about being disloyal to your friends.'

'I can't imagine what I saw in him now. But at the time I was madly in love, and I didn't have as much time for Hannah as I usually did. I should have probed her more about the text thing. By the time she did tell me about it, it was too late. I'll never forgive myself for that.' Our eyes meet, and I give her a sympathetic smile.

'Did you see the text that arrived while she was in your room?' I ask.

'No, she wouldn't show me her phone. You know what she was like, said she respected this person and didn't want to embarrass them.'

'How do you know she wasn't lying?' Theo asks. 'Obviously I didn't know her, but I'm just putting this out there.'

'Hannah wasn't like that; she was a good person,' Kat says.

'Tell me about it.' Daisy rolls her eyes.

'From what I've picked up so far,' Theo says, 'there's a lot you don't know about her.'

'She *was* a good person,' Amy says, as if she's trying to convince herself.

Nobody says anything for a while. I've barely mentioned Hannah to Theo. What has Daisy been telling him?

'Did anybody else know anything about this?' Kat asks eventually. 'Because I didn't.' We all shake our heads.

'I reported it to the police – I assume they checked her phone.'

'It was never found,' Sam says. 'Until now, that is. I know, because they thought I had it. Unless they were bluffing, but if so, they did a pretty good job.'

'Right,' Kat says. 'I think it's time to move on.' She's definitely sobered up. I can't help wondering whether she hammed it up a bit to get us to play the game. But why would she do that?

'Daisy,' she says. 'It's your turn next.'

CHAPTER TWENTY

Daisy's focus is on the carpet, as if she wishes it were a flying carpet that could sail her out of here, out of this moment. I can't see her without imagining her with Theo. I drink some wine. I sense Theo is watching me, but I focus on Daisy, keep my face composed. The wine slips down my throat and stokes my fire.

'Do we really have to do this? It's not easy for me.' She looks up, her eyes flashing, daring us to contradict her. 'Nothing to do with having something to hide, but embarrassing. I stole Sam from the golden girl.'

'Maybe not so golden,' Sam says. 'Let's be real here. We said when we started that this wasn't going to be comfortable. I knew Hannah better than any of you and she could be hard work.'

Kat puts her hand on Daisy's arm.

'We're old friends here. You and Sam – look at you. Married for goodness knows how many years, with two beautiful children. What happened back then with you and Hannah, we're all over it. Tell us what happened. Just so we can get a clearer picture. Whatever you remember might help.'

'OK.' Daisy shakes the ice and fruit around in her glass with her slender fingers, perfect red nails. 'The last time I saw Hannah wasn't great. It was at a party over in one of the other halls – the ones that were slightly further out of campus, a bit smarter than ours … What were they called?'

'Highfield,' Sam says.

'That's it. I always wished I lived there. The rooms were so much bigger. The party was held by someone I didn't know, but a guy on my course invited me, and although I hadn't arranged to go with Sam, he was there with his mates. Do you remember?'

'Of course I do,' Sam says. 'I wish I didn't. Some guy got completely out of it and threw up in a vegetable patch out the back. Decorated the cabbages.'

'Gross,' Daisy says. 'I don't remember that.'

'The warden got involved and everything the next day.'

'So Hannah was at the party?' Kat asks.

'Yes, unfortunately,' Daisy says. 'If I'd known she was going to be there, I would never have gone. She knew about me and Sam by then, but I didn't want to rub it in her face no matter what you all thought at the time.' Again her eyes flash at us, accusatory.

'We didn't—' Amy says.

Daisy holds her hand up to stop her. 'Yes, you did. It's fine, I'm over it. I'm just telling it how it was. Sam and I had a few drinks, started dancing, had a bit of a smooch and were getting quite into one another – you know how it is – when Hannah appeared. She was just watching me with those big eyes of hers.' Her gaze flicks towards the photo, and she scowls. 'If anyone knew how to make a person feel guilty, it was her. She had that vulnerable air about her, like a fragile doll that might break if handled roughly. It was unnerving, and I tried to ignore her because I didn't want to make a scene. But she approached me, said she wanted to talk. We went out into the garden and she asked me when I'd got together with Sam.'

Sam groans and puts his head in his hands.

'Do we have to do this? It was so long ago.'

'Please, Sam,' Amy says. 'It might help.'

'You said you were OK with it earlier,' Kat says.

'Yeah, but—'

'Go on, Daisy.'

Daisy glares at Sam's bent head.

'Up until then, she thought we hadn't overlapped. We'd let her think that, but I prefer to tell it how it is. I'd had a couple of drinks and I'd had enough. I put her straight. Told her we'd been seeing each other for a couple of weeks before they split up. That's all it was. Don't look at me like that, Sam – you hated cheating on her. I could see it was tearing you apart, and I think being truthful is the best option.'

'How did she take it?' Amy asks.

'Not well. She said some nasty things to me, like how I was just using Sam and he'd soon see through me. I said it was up to Sam who he wanted to go out with, and she kind of wilted like a flower in front of me, because she knew he wouldn't choose her. It was horrible; believe me, the last thing I wanted to do was hurt her, despite the vicious things she'd said. Luckily some girl came out at that point to see where she was, and I went back inside, grabbed Sam and got him out of there.'

'What girl?' I ask.

'How am I supposed to know?'

'Seems a bit convenient to me.' My fists are clenched tightly. 'Hannah was never *nasty*, as you put it. She wasn't like that.'

'You don't know what she was like,' Daisy says. 'That much is pretty clear.'

'We're still playing truth or dare,' Amy says. 'I have to assume you're all telling the truth. And it might make us feel uncomfortable' – she looks at me – 'but that's all part of the game.' She addresses Daisy. 'So she didn't actually speak to Sam?'

'No.' Sam and Daisy speak in unison.

Everyone is silent.

'It must be hard for you,' Amy says, 'if that was the last time you spoke, arguing like that.'

Daisy stirs the straw around her glass, ice clinking softly. 'I hate it, I wish it could be different. I wish Hannah was here to see it wasn't a cheap affair, but the start of something real. True love.' She looks up and locks eyes with Sam, and they share a moment. Then she breaks the gaze. 'She looked at me as if I was some kind of floozy taking her man away just because I could. If only she could see me and Sam now, see how long we've lasted.'

'Maybe she can,' Amy says.

'Nice of you, Amy, but I don't believe in all that after-life claptrap. And that picture up there is spooking me out. Those eyes have been on me all night. Just like they were at that bloody party. And some party this is,' Daisy adds.

'I told you it wasn't exactly a party.'

'Whatever you want to call it, it should be fun. I can't believe you're making us bring all this stuff up. I've tried to scrub that evening from my memory.'

'It's hard, I know. Bear with me, please, all of you. This is important. I'm determined to find out what happened to Hannah.'

'That's me done, anyway. I'm going to the bathroom before the next person has their turn.'

She leaves the room. Sam and Theo start talking and I take advantage of the moment to speak to Amy.

'I can't believe Daisy is making Hannah out to be so awful.'

She plays with her nails as she speaks, not looking at me.

'I think she's telling the truth.'

'Even the part where she said Hannah made nasty comments about her? Hannah was never cruel, and I can't imagine her standing up to Daisy like that.'

'Maybe she'd had a drink.'

Given what Amy told me earlier about her jealousy towards Hannah, she must be letting it affect her opinion. I wish I could tell her why I know Daisy is capable of telling lies, but even now, despite the game, it's not my truth to reveal, and I have to respect her wishes. As for her and Theo – I'm waiting for the right moment.

I go into the kitchen to top up my wine, and Theo follows me. He touches my arm and I move away.

'I thought you weren't drinking,' he says.

'I changed my mind. All this game stuff, it's not easy. And you aren't exactly helping.'

'What do you mean?'

'Playing devil's advocate. Are you sure that's all this is? Or is there something I should know?'

'Of course not.' He fiddles with his shirt button. 'It's fine, have a drink. I'm sure one night won't hurt. It can't be easy finding out your friend might have been murdered. Let's hope the killer isn't amongst us, eh?'

I pretend to laugh, hating him, looking back at the group I've known for so long. But he's got me thinking. A couple of hours ago, I thought I knew Theo, but look how wrong I was. How well do I really know any of these people?

CHAPTER TWENTY-ONE

Kat sips at her orange juice, a wicked gleam in her eye. Whatever the reason, at least she's eased off the booze. I can't work her out this evening. The game is making me feel uncomfortable and fascinated at the same time. Why isn't she feeling the same? Is it because she's the puppet master? It's her game and her rules and we're all playing along. But she's doing it for Hannah, like we all are. Isn't she? A sliver of doubt hovers in the back of my mind. I'm next in the circle and dread is settling in my stomach.

'Your turn, Louise.' Everyone shifts about and settles, and I wish my throat didn't feel so tight. Theo has squeezed back into the circle and is sitting on the floor between me and Daisy. Daisy is sipping a gin and tonic and looks more composed now. Sam comes back in from the garden, where he'd popped out for a cigarette. I sip at my wine, gripping the glass, and my stomach churns with anxiety, knowing I'm going to have to reveal something that might not go down well with everyone. Something I've never shared with anyone, not even Amy. I steel myself. It can't have been easy for Daisy either.

I wonder whether I should tell them about the penultimate time I saw Hannah. It was five days before she went missing. We'd been for a run together and then showered at the sports centre and got the bus into town. We'd been for a drink at the campus bar the previous night, and her mood had dipped with each sip of lager she took. By the third glass, tears were sliding down her face.

'I'm not coping,' she'd said, those doe eyes beseeching me for some kind of release from her pain. 'Each morning I wake up with Sam on my mind, and I can't get him out of my head. I took it all for granted, you know, happiness, the way we fitted together and lived our lives. It never occurred to me that one day it would stop. I had a future planned already, marriage, kids; maybe not immediately, but I assumed it would happen one day. It hurts, Lou' – she'd jabbed at her chest – 'in here, deep inside. It's a physical pain and it's taken me over. I can't think or eat or study. At the rate I'm going, I won't get a degree either. I'll leave university with no qualification and no life partner. Because that's what I thought he was; me and Sam, for life. I hadn't considered any other possibility.'

I'd told her I wished I could help take that pain away, but to be honest, my experience with relationships was limited back then – the one break-up I'd endured had been a huge relief. Fred and I had been seeing one another for six months during the second year. He was a history and politics student I'd met at a campus party, and the attraction was immediate, the first few weeks a heady mixture of lust and not a lot else. That soon faded, and we carried on but it was half-hearted on both sides. Hence the relief when he had texted me to end it – yes, texted – was instant. Sure, I'd missed having someone to hang out with, but it was nothing to what Hannah was enduring. We'd all thought she and Sam were soulmates, hadn't we?

She had regurgitated the whole sorry tale about Sam and Daisy; I already knew it, but I could see it helped her to thrash it out, to get it out of her system. She'd perked up a bit by the end of the night and had organised some counselling. Another reason I never saw her as suicidal – who makes future plans if they're not planning on having a future?

I turn my focus back to the group, where the others wait expectantly.

'The last time I saw her – apart from at the Brontë lecture which you all know about –was when Hannah and I were in town, walking along the main road towards the shopping centre. I noticed Sam and Daisy coming towards us, but on the other side of the road. I tried to distract Hannah by pointing out something in a shop window, but I was too slow and she'd already seen them. She was visibly upset, so we ditched the shopping and went straight to a pub and had a drink instead. She couldn't bear seeing Sam with someone else – or at least that's what I thought, but then she told me …' I stop to take in some air, anxious about the reaction I'm going to get. 'She said Sam had been messaging her for the last couple of days and she was really confused because it was making it harder to let go. It made her think they still had a future.'

'What?' Daisy sits up and looks at Sam, then back at me. 'This is bullshit. Tell her, Sam.'

'What kind of messages?' Sam asks.

'Asking her to meet up, that was the gist of it, as far as I can remember. And she'd been thinking about agreeing to it as she desperately wanted to get back with you and had convinced herself you must have split with Daisy. So seeing the two of you in town together shattered her dreams. Again.' I can't resist the last little dig, avoid looking at Amy, knowing she'll disapprove. After what she just told me, I'm no longer sure she's on Hannah's side.

'It's not true,' Sam says. 'I wouldn't do that. I didn't send her any messages.'

'You'd better not have,' Daisy says.

'What?' Sam's jaw is clenched tight. 'Let's not go there, Daisy.'

I squirm around in my seat, but I can't stop now. 'The thing is, Sam, she showed me her phone. I saw the texts.'

'They weren't from me,' Sam says. 'Look, let's not jump to conclusions. There has to be an explanation.'

'Her phone was never found,' Daisy says. 'Convenient, that.' She runs her tongue over her lips. 'Until today.'

'Please don't argue,' Amy says. 'We all agreed to play. It was never going to be easy. And it's what I wanted – tonight is all about Hannah.'

'I'm just telling you what I saw. Hannah was very mixed up at the time. She was hugely anxious about her exams and I was worried she was going to have some kind of breakdown. She was clearly bothered about something and I sensed she wasn't telling me everything. The last time I saw her was at the Brontë lecture the afternoon she disappeared. She wasn't herself at all and rushed off the second it ended. I'll never forgive myself for not going after her.'

'Other students witnessed her there too,' Daisy says. 'It was in the news.'

I'm not sure why she feels the need to point this out. Does she think I'm lying?

'I know. And shortly afterwards, she was seen near a van.'

'Did anyone witness her getting into the van?' Jade asks.

'Not exactly. A witness saw her walking alongside a white van. The van may have had nothing to do with it,' Sam says. 'But I had a van at the time, which meant I came under a lot of scrutiny. So frustrating for me.'

'But if the police asked you about it earlier, they must think it's relevant,' I say.

'Who knows?' He swigs from his beer. 'I hope they do get to the bottom of it.'

He should be careful what he wishes for; now the game has started I'm scared of where it might lead.

'That's exactly why I wanted to do this,' Amy says. 'I've wanted to get this group together for a long time, and it's finally happening.'

There's a strange glint in her eye when she says this, and for a flicker of a moment I wonder if she's planned this all along. Has she downplayed her jealousy of Hannah? Or is she in cahoots with

Kat? Is the game a set-up? Whatever is going on, I don't want it to stop. It feels as if we are getting closer to Hannah and the truth. What else will be uncovered along the way?

Blackwood Independent, 15 October 2005

A verdict of suicide was reached yesterday at the inquest into the death of Hannah Robinson, 21, of Kenilworth, Warwickshire. Beloved Buckinghamshire University student Hannah was found dead in Blackwood Forest in April. The English student was in the final year of her degree course and disappeared shortly before her exams. A long-term relationship had recently ended, and she was said to be distraught, as well as suffering the pressure of exams and living up to the expectation that she would get a first-class degree. Hannah's family were too upset to comment.

CHAPTER TWENTY-TWO

The back door is open and the wind has picked up outside, making the tea lights around the room flicker and flare. Sam pushes the door to and turns the music up. I've been so engrossed in the game I hadn't noticed it was even playing. The track has a pulsing beat and makes me picture a heart pumping in and out, the way mine is thumping hard in my chest, as if it has to work extra hard to keep up.

I'm trying to figure out from everybody's expressions what they make of my account. The circle we're sitting in and the tea lights and the weird atmosphere make it feel like a seance, which in a way it almost is. We're just trying to reach Hannah through our own memories of her, rather than with a Ouija board and wobbling tables. Where I'm sitting, opposite the photo of Hannah, her striking eyes have been watching me all evening. Her eyes were always the most noticeable thing about her: large, and so expressive whatever her mood. Immortalised aged twenty-one, she'll forever be one of those people destined never to grow old. But just how well did we really know her? This evening her gaze seems to be beseeching me to get this right, and the responsibility presses down on me. I want to hang on to the Hannah I thought I knew, not this different Hannah who appears to be emerging this evening. A scene flashes into my memory: Hannah's face twisted and distorted with anger, an image I've suppressed.

Theo is refreshing drinks, and despite the alcohol, the game has had a sobering effect. After each person has finished speaking, there's an aftermath, each of us shutting down with our thoughts.

Despite the name of the game, how do we know people are telling the truth? Given the looks Sam is giving me, he's convinced I'm not. He notices me watching him.

'How do we know you're telling the truth?' he asks.

Mind-reader.

I shrug. 'You can't know. What about you? Did you send those text messages?'

He looks into my eyes in a way that makes me believe him. Does he know? I wonder. Somehow I don't think he does.

'No, I swear. What I said earlier was the truth. If I had sent them, I'd have owned up to it. We've already argued about it. I can't see what possible good can come of this.'

'We need a lie detector test,' says Daisy.

'Seriously?' Kat says, shaking her head.

Amy, who has moved to sitting cross-legged on the floor, folds her legs underneath her and kneels up.

'We're Hannah's oldest friends. If we can't trust one another, we might as well stop the game. We can't afford to do that. If there's a chance we're all telling the truth – and I, for one, believe you all are – then we need to look at all these accounts together and see if we can piece together what happened to her. Try and put aside any grievances and preconceptions and let's lay it all out and see what we've got. Louise learned of those messages from Hannah, who told her they were from Sam. I believe her. Sam ... no, Sam let me finish ... Sam says he didn't send them and I believe him too. So who did send them? Do you see? Maybe somebody used his phone to make it seem as if the messages were coming from him. When we thought it was suicide, it seemed plausible that Hannah might have destroyed her phone, not wanting anyone to read her personal messages, but now we know what's happened to it, that clearly wasn't the case. Let's put everything on the table and then make our judgements. It's not meant to be comfortable. We all want the same result here. It's Sam's go next.'

'OK,' Kat says. 'Over to you, Sam. What happened when you last saw Hannah?'

Sam is on the sofa, next to Daisy. While she is sitting back against a cushion, he is perched on the edge, as if about to take flight. He's holding a bottle of beer and staring into it. He goes to speak, takes Daisy's hand instead and squeezes it. 'I love you, Daisy,' he says.

He drops her hand. 'The last time I saw Hannah was the occasion Louise mentioned just now. I was in town with my mates and Daisy. Daisy and I were holding hands. It was early days for us, and hate me for it if you want, but she was all I could think about. I was twenty, a hot-blooded young man, falling in love with a beautiful woman.'

Daisy's smile is smug and I'm seething. Sam wipes sweat from his face with his hand and continues.

'My mates were walking behind us when suddenly Daisy said, "Oh, no," and there she was, Hannah, across the way with Lou, and I wanted to be anywhere but there. Her hair looked lank, and that really hit me, as she used to take such care of her hair when we were together. I hated knowing it was me who'd made her feel bad about herself. I hoped she wouldn't spot us, but she looked over at me and stopped right there on the pavement. Lou saw us too and pulled her aside, and then the moment was gone. That was my last time and I wish it wasn't. I'll never forget that look.' He drinks from his bottle. 'But it wasn't the last time we spoke.'

Daisy's head jerks up.

'I felt really shit about it, so I called her the next day to say sorry. The way she'd found out about us was horrible, and I needed to tell her she deserved better. But she surprised me by saying she was fine about it, considering, and we had a conversation. She wished me and Daisy well and said that seeing us together was difficult but with time she'd be OK. She said she missed talking to me and asked if we could meet up, as she had a problem she couldn't tell anyone else about. She said talking to me would help.

'I said it wasn't a good idea to meet, as it wasn't fair on Daisy. That was the wrong thing to say, and I realised it was only bravado making her claim she was fine with us being over, because she started crying and said she couldn't carry on like this.'

His fingertips are white where he's clutching the beer, and he squeezes his eyes shut.

'I'm sorry I never told you, but I couldn't bear to bring it up. We've worked so hard to put it behind us.'

Daisy reaches over and takes his free hand.

'It's all right, babe. This is so hard, I know.' She looks around the circle. 'Sam felt terrible after that call, as you can imagine, especially when she took her own life.'

'*If* she took her own life,' Amy says. A tea light flickers behind her, casting a shadow on the wall. 'What do you think, Sam?'

'I think she was desperate. Desperate enough to kill herself? Yes, I thought so at the time, but the police say otherwise, so …' He spreads his hands out.

'What do you think was bothering her? Did she give you any clues?'

'*Somebody* was bothering her. That's how she put it. I thought, like you said, Lou, that it must be that Mark guy, as she'd mentioned before that he was keen on her, but she'd said it in a jokey way, so at the time I didn't get the impression it bothered her.'

My stomach sinks and I can't look at Kat. Jade, twisting her bangles around her wrist, catches my eye again.

'And what about the texts she told Louise you sent?'

'It wasn't me, I swear. What would I do that for? Everything was difficult enough as it was without giving her false hope. That would have been cruel. It's not my style, either. Like I said, I rang her.'

'Did you tell the police all this?'

'Of course. I told them back then and I told them yesterday. But all they were interested in yesterday was the van. The problem is, there are so many white vans around.'

He looks around at us one by one. 'I messed up, and I'm sorry for hurting Hannah. But it's ancient history. That Hannah' – he points at the photo on the mantelpiece – 'would be over all this if she was still alive, and she'd hate for us to be feeling bad so long after the event. You know how caring she was, how important her friends were to her. She'd want us all to move on, I reckon. After this game is done, that's what we should do. For Hannah.'

Jade clears her throat. 'Obviously I didn't know her, but if it was me, I'd want my friends to find out who murdered me. What do you think?' she asks Kat.

Kat nods. 'Well said.'

'From what I've heard tonight, I don't think any of us could say we knew Hannah,' Daisy says.

'I knew her,' Sam says. 'You might hate me for saying it, but I wish I'd never met her. And I bet I'm not the only one.'

I hate to admit he's right.

'Did you tell the police that as well?' Kat asks.

Sam scowls. 'Of course not. I'm amongst friends here, aren't I?'

Silence fills the next few seconds, until Amy jumps in.

'Of course.'

'Well that's all you're getting from me. I need another drink and some fresh air, and then it's your turn, Kat. See how you like it. Let's get this over with.'

It's time for Kat to answer the question: what happened the last time you saw Hannah? But will she tell us the truth? Or will she miss something out like I did?

CHAPTER TWENTY-THREE

Nobody says much until Sam returns from the garden. Jade takes Kat's hand and pulls her down onto the sofa.

Kat clears her throat and Jade passes her a glass of water.

'Kat,' Daisy says. 'What happened the last time you saw Hannah?'

Kat grips the glass of water tightly, addresses her words to Amy.

'I first met Hannah at your flat. You'd told me she was the quiet one amongst your group, the complete opposite to me. I wasn't sure we'd have a lot in common, from what you'd said. She wanted to be a university lecturer and was never without a book on the go. I was enjoying my art course, but the social life was more important to me, especially that first year. From what Amy had said, Hannah spent more time in the library than the bar on campus; I barely knew where the library was. Suffice to say my expectations weren't high, but there was something about her that captivated me. That first evening she barely noticed me; it was Sam who got her attention, and she spent the whole evening engrossed with him.

'But there was something about her. She was so neat, with her snub nose and flyaway hair, and the way she sat on the floor, gazing at Sam ...' She drinks some water, hesitates, looks at the carpet. 'I wanted her gaze to be fixed on me in the same way.' Her cheeks flush with colour. 'So although we didn't have much interaction that night, I was sure we had a connection – she just hadn't had a chance to discover it yet.

'But then Sam became serious for her and I tried to put her out of my mind, but I never could. The next best thing happened and we became a close-knit group of friends, and she and I developed a special bond, like Amy had with both Lou and Daisy, and that was enough. I could see she wasn't interested in me and only had eyes for Sam. I told myself it was a crush and I'd get over it.

'And then the unthinkable happened. We all had Hannah and Sam married off, didn't we? But once the furore over Sam and Daisy getting together had died down, I could see they were much better suited, though I could never say this at the time – to any of you, let alone Hannah. I mean, look how they've lasted.' She glances at Daisy when she says this, and Daisy gives her one of her special smiles that make you feel like you're basking in sunlight.

'Hannah was devastated, of course, and I was there for her whenever she wanted. She'd ring me during the night, sobbing, and I always answered; it made me feel valued and special, and she came to rely on me. Before I knew it, we were spending time together every day, and she'd call me before she went to sleep at night. My feelings for her came back like a whirlwind, sweeping me up and carrying me away. It got so that I knew I'd have to tell her, because it was killing me; more importantly, I could tell she was falling for me too. Little things she'd say, a gesture, a touch. And then one night when we were on the phone, she came out with it: "I love you, Kat." I'm sure my heart stopped, and I said, "I love you too, Hannah, I've always loved you." She didn't speak after that, and I wondered if she was bursting with happiness like I was, but as the silence grew, fear crept along the line and seized me by the throat. At last she whispered, "I don't mean ... Oh, Kat ... that isn't what I meant at all," and hung up.

'I couldn't reach her after that. I rang again and again but she wouldn't pick up, so early the next morning I went round to her flat. She wouldn't let me in her room. She called the warden and he asked me to leave. The humiliation. And after that she was always with someone else – usually you, Amy, but often her friends from her course – so I couldn't speak to her on my own. I knew I should never have said anything. I'd misjudged her feelings and made a terrible mistake.

'The worst thing was she wouldn't let me apologise. I wrote her a letter and left it in her pigeonhole, and she posted it back unopened. Emails weren't answered and she never responded to my texts. When I did see her across campus, I could tell she wasn't happy – she'd got thinner, and her face was pale, her hair hanging around her face like string. She used to take such good care of her hair. I knew it wasn't me that had done that to her, but my timing was bad, what with all the other things going on in her life.

'I texted her every day. It was important to stay in touch, and I didn't want her to forget me. I knew she'd come round. And then suddenly she started replying to my messages, like I'd known she would. And she wanted to meet.

'I suggested she come over to my room, or me to hers, but she said she wanted to meet down by the sports centre after she'd been to running club. When I got there, she was wearing jeans and a sweatshirt and she hadn't got a bag, so it didn't look like she'd been running at all. In hindsight I reckon she wanted us to meet somewhere neutral, outside, and that made me feel awful, like she saw me as some sort of threat. We went for a walk and she apologised for blanking me for so long, but she needed space to think all her problems over – not just me, but the split with Sam and falling out with Daisy. She was tormented by the fact that she might lose a friend as well as a partner. The conversation was awkward at first, but that didn't last long. It was cold that day and she was only wearing that thin jacket she used to wear all the time; her lips were going blue, so I suggested we go for a coffee, and she was all right with that.

'She really missed you, Daisy; that was the first thing she said when we sat down. All her worries tumbled out in a torrent. She hadn't done any revision because she couldn't concentrate. She couldn't concentrate because she couldn't sleep. She couldn't sleep because all she could think about was Sam. I said I'd thought she was getting over it – we all did. Do you remember how after about a month she was back interacting with us, more subdued but more like her old self – the Hannah we all used to rely on for notes. She said she had been feeling better, but then Sam had texted her asking to meet, and that had set her anxiety off again and she didn't know what to do. She wanted to see him, but only if he wanted to get back together with her, which she thought he did.

'I told her to be careful, and she said no disrespect, but how did she know I didn't have an ulterior motive. That was when we moved on to talk about me and her. She asked if I was still in love with her, and I didn't know what to say. I was, but I didn't want to frighten her off; her friendship was so important to me, and I was scared of losing her. I mentally tossed a coin and took a risk. Bad move. I confessed my feelings and she listened. When I'd finished, she said she was sorry I'd got the wrong idea and she thought it better if we didn't see each other for a while, so that I could forget her. She assured me she was doing the right thing for me, but I was devastated and humiliated and I begged her to reconsider. She left at that point and I was furious with myself for opening up to her.'

'I bet you were angry with her, too,' Daisy says.

Kat shrugs.

'When was this?' Amy asks.

'It was two days before she disappeared.' Kat finishes her water, rubs her eyes. 'All this time we thought it was suicide and I blamed myself. I thought it was my fault.'

'You did nothing wrong,' Jade says. 'We can't help who we fall in love with.'

'Exactly,' says Daisy, although she looks sceptical. 'Thanks for sharing that, Kat; it means a lot to me to know she was sad about our friendship. It wasn't easy for me, falling for Sam. I knew how much she cared about him and I tried to stay away. We fought it for ages, didn't we?'

Sam nods.

'I feel so stupid for getting the wrong idea about her,' Kat says. 'It was all wishful thinking on my part. But I couldn't get her out of my head. I was frantic when she stopped speaking to me. I've never got over it. It made me wary of letting myself get too close to others – I was convinced they'd push me away, like she had. My self-worth was non-existent. If you want out, Jade, I understand totally. I'd walk away now if I were you.'

Jade squeezes her arm.

'You were so young. And times were different then. Hannah didn't know how to deal with it, that's all. I'm sure she'd have come round in the end; she wouldn't have wanted to lose a good friend like you.'

Kat's eyes fill with tears and she blinks them away.

'Do you really think so?'

Jade nods.

'I need a drink after that.'

'Come on,' Jade says. 'I'll get you one.'

'So it's true,' Daisy says to Sam. 'You *were* texting Hannah. Kat just confirmed it. What's going on? You're lying, admit it. Hannah told both Louise and Kat that you'd been in touch with her.'

Sam looks incredulous. 'I've already told you, I did *not* send Hannah any texts. The rest of you believe me, don't you?'

I play with the button on my sleeve to avoid looking at him. I don't know what to believe any more.

'I don't understand why Hannah would lie. Unless, as Amy said earlier, somebody pretended to be you.'

'Which is what must have happened.'

'Maybe,' Daisy says.

'Christ! If you don't believe me, what chance have I got? Amy, what do you think?'

'I agree that somebody must have wanted it to look as if you were sending them. The question is why.'

'To wind me up,' Daisy says. 'Which is why I think Hannah was making it up.'

'That's possible,' I say. 'But another possibility is that someone wanted to make Hannah think Sam was still interested.'

Amy glances over to the kitchen, where Jade and Kat are talking.

'I didn't want to say this in front of Kat,' she says, her voice lowered, 'but I can't be the only one thinking it. The unwanted admirer Hannah told me about, who was harassing her, do you think she meant Kat?'

The faces in front of me are serious now, as they all contemplate the idea that has been hovering in my mind and what this could mean. What if Kat is lying? What if she pushed Hannah too far?

CHAPTER TWENTY-FOUR

'She kept that well hidden,' Amy says. 'I had no idea. Do you think she told the police?'

I shake my head. 'I suspect not. But what was the motive behind not telling them? Not wanting to out herself? I know she was out to us lot, but telling the police is on a whole other level.'

'Or because she had something else to hide?'

'She didn't have to tell us. And if Jade hadn't been here, maybe she wouldn't have done.'

'What do you mean?'

Amy deserves the truth. I push my reservations to one side.

'All these years her feelings for Hannah have been holding her back, have stopped her getting close to anyone else. Now she's met Jade, she wants to be able to forget.'

'So that's why she started this game,' Daisy says. 'Makes sense.'

'Something like that. She's ashamed.'

'What if it was more than that?' Sam says.

'What do you mean?' Amy asks.

'I shouldn't say.'

'Look, you're not going to be feeling comfortable, we all get that. We knew the game might throw up some difficult truths. Just tell us.'

'OK.' He takes a deep breath. 'What if she felt so strongly that she wanted to punish Hannah?'

'It was Kat's idea to play the game in the first place. Why would she do that?'

'She's been on edge since we got here. She was drinking, which she isn't used to. Who knows? I'm just putting it out there as a possibility. Just suppose for a minute Kat had something to do with Hannah's death; making up the messages from me makes sense, or sending them herself to punish Hannah, to lure her into something.'

I feel sick at the thought that Kat could have hurt Hannah. Equally, Sam could be shifting the blame away from himself.

'Let's get her back in here,' Daisy says. 'She started this game off; she can't just abandon it.'

She calls Kat and Jade through.

'Jade's given me a slightly different version of what you told us back there, and I want to know the truth,' I say. 'Were you and Hannah in a relationship?'

She shakes her head, defeated. 'I wanted to be. We got very close, things happened, and then … She was interested, let's just say I could tell.'

'It must have been hard keeping that to yourself.'

'You get used to it.'

'Did you know about this, Sam?'

'No. No offence, Kat, but Hannah wasn't into women.'

'How would you know?' Kat says.

'She was my girlfriend.'

'You obviously didn't know her very well. Hannah didn't know what she wanted.'

'Tell us what happened between you then.'

They lock eyes.

'It's private,' she says.

'We waived all rights to privacy when we agreed to play the game.'

'All right! I kissed her and she responded. There, satisfied now?' She brushes her forearm across her eyes, not wanting to show she's upset.

'I don't believe you,' Sam says.

'Sam.' Amy frowns. 'We gave you the benefit of the doubt.'

Sam scowls at the carpet.

'Why didn't you talk to me or Amy; why keep it to yourself?' I ask, wanting to defuse the situation.

'Pride. Embarrassment. People not believing me. But I'm glad it's out in the open.'

'Is that the end of the game?' Jade asks.

'We should all discuss what's happened so far,' Amy says. 'But let's have a quick break first. Lou, come with me.'

I follow her into the garden.

'What's up?'

'I just wanted a breather. It's pretty full-on – throwing up so much I didn't know about.'

'Isn't it? Daisy wasn't best pleased when Sam mentioned calling Hannah, was she? I feel sorry for him, actually; it felt like he was being really honest during the game. It can't have been easy for him. Although after turning on Kat like that, I'm not sure he deserves my sympathy.'

'I know what you mean. It can't have been easy for you either. It must have been hard saying all that in front of Sam – and Daisy.'

'It was, but I'm like you – this has obsessed me for a long time and it feels good to get it all out in the open. You've absolutely done the right thing.'

'Thanks. I'm not sure the others would agree. I can't work out why Kat initiated this game.' Amy shifts her gaze from my face, and hesitates.

'What is it?'

She sighs. 'You left something out of your account about Hannah.'

A cold feeling takes hold of me.

'No I didn't.' *She knows.*

'Hannah told me about the essay.'

The cold feeling intensifies. I can't believe she'd break her promise. Clearly I didn't know her at all. 'It had nothing to do with the last time I saw her; that's why I didn't mention it.'

'You don't need to be defensive. I wish you'd told me, that's all.'

'We had such a horrible argument. I'd never seen her so angry. And I was ashamed, like Kat, only I didn't have the guts to tell you all.'

I'll never forget the humiliation of that afternoon in Professor Galloway's office. Normally such an affable man, his manner had completely changed. He'd called me in to speak about my essay grade. When I arrived, I was surprised to see Hannah sitting outside. Her face was drawn; I'd got used to that since her split with Sam, but she wouldn't look me in the eye.

Professor Galloway called us in and told us our essays followed the same argument and were almost identical, and that he was going to fail them both on account of plagiarism, unless we could come up with an explanation. I had to confess that I'd borrowed Hannah's notes and the books she'd used for the assignment, as I had missed a week's classes due to illness. I'd struggled with the topic but had managed to write my essay, and hadn't thought anything of it.

I told him it was purely coincidental, and that if fault was to be found then it was with me, and that Hannah should not be penalised. Hannah barely said a word. I was mortified that this could have happened, and being labelled a cheat made me want to die with shame. He sent us away telling us he'd let us know his decision within a week.

Hannah asked me to go back to her room and we had a terrible argument. She said I'd humiliated her and if she failed to get a first it was all my fault and she'd make me pay. I'd never seen her so angry before, and the worst thing was she didn't believe I had made a genuine mistake. That upset me more than Professor Galloway's reaction. In the end, Hannah was exonerated and I had to resubmit the essay.

'Hannah apologised for what she'd said, and I was so relieved, but hated myself for adding to her stress at such a difficult time. Can you imagine if she hadn't got a first on top of losing Sam? This only happened two weeks before she died. It's so embarrassing, but she promised not to tell anyone. I can't believe she told you. Did I even know her at all? After this evening, I'm not so sure.'

'I didn't think for a minute you'd cheated,' Amy says, 'and thanks for telling me.'

'It's fine; to be honest, I've got a lot more on my mind right now. Theo—'

'Sam's here,' Amy says. 'You OK, Sam?'

'I can't find the bottle opener.'

'Let me show you. We'll chat more later, Lou.'

My emotions are all over the place, and seeing Daisy joking with Theo when I re-join the group doesn't help.

'Let's go over what we've discovered so far,' says Amy, sitting back down.

'I need a drink first,' Daisy says. 'Theo, will you get me one?'

She holds out her glass and their fingers touch as he takes it from her. Something inside me snaps and I see how the game can help me.

'He's not the waiter, you know. Just because he made a few cocktails. Why can't you get it yourself?'

'It's OK,' Theo says. 'I don't mind.' My cheeks burn that he's taking her side.

'Well hurry up, because the game isn't finished.'

'Isn't it?' Daisy says. 'We've all had a turn.'

'Wait a sec,' Theo says. 'Just getting myself a beer too.'

You'll need it. The smile I give him masks the contempt I'm feeling for him.

'Here's a bottle.' He holds it out to me.

'Cheers.' Why not go through the motions? Lull him into a false sense of security. It's no more than he deserves. Deep down

I know this is foolhardy, but I'm blinded by anger and nothing can divert me from what I'm about to do.

Everyone is roughly back in the circle as before. I'm standing in the middle with the bottle and Daisy is stroking her glossy hair, and for a split second I imagine bashing the bottle down on her head. Intrusive, devilish thoughts. Everyone must get them. I grip it hard against my side. Music is still playing in the background and eyes are watching me expectantly.

I crouch down in the middle and put the bottle on the carpet, then turn towards Theo.

'I don't really need this bottle, as there's only one question that needs answering here. Obviously it's not the Hannah question. This one is for you, Theo. Who's not such an outsider after all.' I spin the bottle and catch it when the neck points towards him. A trail of red wine spills on the carpet. Theo shifts about and frowns at me.

'What's going on, Lou?' His eyes dart to the faces of the others, but he won't find answers there.

'This is a truth, not a dare, and I want you to think about the question very carefully.'

Daisy is to my left; I can see her out of the corner of my eye. Her gaze is fixed on me and she's very still. The music is no longer playing. I stand up and look down at Theo, enjoying the surge of power I feel, then risk a look at Daisy before I ask the question that everyone is waiting to hear.

'Tell me the name of the woman you were sleeping with last year.'

The room is absolutely silent as Theo and I lock eyes and I see incredulity turning into anger and then fear.

'What?'

I hold his gaze.

'Why are you doing this here, now, in front of your friends?' He looks at the others as if pleading for help, to get them on side.

'Please, not now, not here. You're making a show of yourself, Lou. Don't do this.'

'I'll repeat the question,' I say. 'Tell me the name of the woman you were sleeping with last year. Or should that be *this* year? I'm not sure I trust anything you've told me any more.'

'What do you mean? Nothing's changed.'

His eyes are fixed on the ground and I bet he wants to look at Daisy, see how she's reacting. I risk a sidelong glance. She's holding her cocktail glass against her face, but I see through that: it's to hide the heat in her cheeks, which will be burning now, showing her for the traitor she is.

'If you can't tell me the truth, then this is the end for us.' He doesn't respond. 'Maybe Daisy might be able to help.' I swivel round to look at her, and she widens her eyes.

'I don't know why you're looking at me like that.'

'Oh come on, Daisy. Have you forgotten your little tête-à-tête with Theo earlier, behind the shed? Did you think nobody would notice? Did you not worry you might be overheard? I'm sure Sam would like to know the answer to my question too.'

Next to Daisy, Amy shifts uncomfortably, and Kat is alert, still, like an animal poised to jump. Heat rushes to my head and I'm hyper-aware that I risk making a fool of myself, but it's too late. Everyone is staring at me, and part of me wishes I could melt into the carpet along with the wine from the bottle.

'What's she talking about?' Sam leans forward to look at Daisy, who can't hide the colour in her cheeks and the dismay in her eyes. She darts a glance at Theo. Amy is shaking her head. Kat and Jade are behind me, so I can't see their reactions. Sam turns his attention to Theo.

'Why don't you answer the question, mate? Louise is right: she's not the only one who wants to know the answer.' He moves away from Daisy so he can see her face. She's biting her lip, avoiding looking at anyone.

Theo's stance has gone from defiant to uncertain.

'Are you sure you want to know the answer?' His voice is barely audible. 'I'm so sorry.'

'Just say it.' Daisy's tone is harsh. 'She obviously knows.'

Amy claps her hand to her mouth.

'I swear it's over,' Theo says. 'I promise—'

'Just say it.' I want this to be over now.

'Daisy. It was Daisy.' As soon as he's said her name, he leaps up and bolts upstairs.

CHAPTER TWENTY-FIVE

Sam grabs his cigarettes and storms out into the garden. Jade and Kat go outside too. Amy gives me a reassuring look, although she can't hide the turmoil in her eyes. Daisy gets up and goes to the kitchen counter, where she pours herself a large drink, trying to mask the slight tremble in her hands as she screws the cap back on the gin.

'Could you give me a few minutes with Louise, please, Amy?' she says.

Amy frowns. 'I'm not sure that's a good idea.'

'It's OK, I'll be fine,' I say. My pulse rate has returned to normal. She squeezes my arm before leaving the room.

Daisy takes a large mouthful of her drink before coming back to the sofa, where she perches on the edge and faces me.

'I'm sorry you had to find out like this, but like Theo said, it's over.'

'How long was it going on for?' Now that it's out in the open, I'm surprisingly calm.

'About seven months. Up until last January.'

That Christmas Day flashes into my head. Theo disappearing after a phone call from his father, the father he barely ever spoke to. The Christmas dinner we had to put on hold for two hours while he went off on a rescue mission. My hungry nephews forced to wait, bickering over their presents, the atmosphere strained and my sister assuring me it was fine, with that pinched look on her face telling me I'd let her down *again*. His upset on his return: his father was sick, didn't have long left, a whole lot of drama over someone he professed not to care about. The miraculous recovery a week later, and he hadn't been to see him since. How could I have been so stupid?

'When did it start?'

'Just after that meal we went on. Theo and I got talking; I was interested in personal training and he gave me his card. This is all my fault, Lou; don't take it out on Theo. Me and Sam – things haven't been right for ages.'

'Are you expecting me to be sympathetic?'

'No of course not, I'm just explaining it. I'll shut up if you'd rather.'

'No, I want to know.' And I do, no matter how much it hurts. I want to hear every sordid detail so that I can know what I'm dealing with here. Whatever made Daisy do it, it takes two, and Theo had his reasons too. Thanks to the therapy, I already know what those are. Everything boils down to the baby issue, which pushes and pulls us in directions we couldn't possibly imagine. And I thought we'd sorted it. An affair with someone I didn't know, I could just about handle, but this? For it to be one of my friends is on a whole other level. And Daisy … I can't see how Theo and I will ever get over this. Or if I want to. And as for having his child … If he were to walk in now, I'd be in danger of doing him serious harm. Better to hear Daisy's side of the story.

'Sam had no idea, did he?' I ask.

She shakes her head. 'We've been having such a tough time. And I'm not just talking recently. Would you believe me if I told you we've had separate bedrooms for five years?'

'Five years?'

She nods, playing with her perfect red nails. Close up, the lines around her eyes are more pronounced than I realised. When she looks up at me, her eyes are full of tears. Despite everything, I feel a pang of sympathy for her.

'And here's me thinking you two had the perfect relationship.'

'Trust me, you have no idea.'

'Seriously, Daisy, I'm not sure I'll trust you ever again.'

She gets up and collects the gin bottle. She tops her glass up and pours some into mine without asking.

'You're going to tell Sam my secret, aren't you?'

'I haven't decided.'

'I realise I can't stop you, but you'd be making a huge mistake.'

'I don't care. What have I got to lose?'

'It wouldn't serve any purpose. I told you, Sam and I are not the perfect couple you think we are. If it wasn't for Hannah, we wouldn't still be together.' Her voice is a little slurred.

'That doesn't make any sense.'

'We stayed together because we had to, not because we loved each other. Oh, we did at first, of course, we were besotted, but it was mostly lust. That wore off eventually, and then we were stuck. He never loved me the way he did Hannah.' Her eyes have a faraway look. Is she picturing Hannah, young and beautiful as she will forever remain in all of our imaginations, while we age and make mistakes and suffer the trials and tribulations of life? That Hannah is never far from my mind, even without the photo Amy has put on display. I wish I could go back to that point where we first met, young and hopeful with the dreams of our lives ahead still a possibility.

Daisy looks around the room, checking we're still alone.

'Theo isn't the first,' she says, lowering her voice in an exaggerated drunken way that means it isn't as quiet as she thinks, though it doesn't matter, as everyone is steering clear of this room. 'Sam knew about the others but not about Theo. I'm not sure what he'll do this time, but he won't leave me; he'll never leave me.'

'Because of the children?'

She shakes her head. 'You wouldn't understand.'

I ignore her patronising remark – it's her and Theo I want to know about, not her and Sam. I don't care about her marriage.

After tonight, I doubt I'll ever speak to either of them again. Amy had good intentions, but this whole birthday reunion was one massive mistake. It's thrown every one of my relationships under the spotlight, and we're all left dealing with the fallout. Even Hannah is no longer who I thought she was.

'When exactly did you and Theo finish?'

'January the first.' She laughs to herself. 'You were his new year's resolution.'

Anger surges through me like a shot of adrenaline.

'You don't care, do you?' I say. 'This conversation isn't about putting things right. And you're kidding yourself about Sam. Didn't you see his reaction back there? He won't stick around after this. Serves you right if he takes the kids with him. You don't deserve them after what you did to him. I don't care what happens to you, Daisy. Face up to what you've done. Your marriage is over.'

'You aren't listening to me,' Daisy says, her eyes laughing, mocking. 'Sam will never leave me, because he can't.'

'You can't know that.' As I'm speaking, I hear someone come into the room behind me, but my eyes are riveted on Daisy's. I can't look away, and I tell myself I will remember this look when I get round to thrashing things out with Theo. It's the ammunition I'll need to drive me.

'Sam will never leave me because I know what he is capable of.'

'Daisy.'

I spin round, shocked. I didn't hear Sam come in. How long has he been there? He steps forward and his tone is harsh, warning. I'm not surprised he doesn't want her sounding off about him like this in public.

'Oh, look who's here,' Daisy says. 'I was just telling Lou how you won't leave me. Because of our agreement.'

'Shut up, you're drunk.'

'I won't shut up. I've had enough and it's time the others know what you did.'

'Daisy, I'm warning you.' Sam steps closer.

'Think about it. This evening is the perfect time to tell them.'

'What are you talking about, Daisy?' I ask. Surely she's not going to tell him about the baby now?

'Tonight. Hannah. You've been asking the wrong question in your stupid game.'

My skin feels cold and I look from Daisy to Sam, not understanding the look of hatred between them.

'What do you mean?'

'Why don't you ask Sam what really happened to Hannah? He wasn't telling the truth when he answered the question earlier. Sam never tells the truth.'

She slams her glass down on the coffee table, triumphant. Gin pools on the glass before dripping onto the floor. Drip, drip, drip.

CHAPTER TWENTY-SIX

'The game isn't finished. Sam's got something to tell you all.' Daisy beckons to Amy, who comes in followed by Kat and Jade. Jade turns to Kat.

'I think I should go.' Alarm distorts her face.

'No, please.' Kat, white-faced, places her hand on Jade's arm. 'I need you here.'

'Sam? What's going on?' Amy asks. 'Were you lying when you answered the question earlier?'

'Come on, Sam,' Daisy says. 'You're not going anywhere until you've told them the truth.'

'Shut up, Daisy,' Sam says. 'She's drunk, she doesn't know what she's talking about.'

'I'm not drunk. I know what I'm saying, and if you won't tell them, I will.'

'Tell us what, Daisy? For fuck's sake. I can't stand this.' Kat glares at her.

'Sam? One last chance.'

Daisy and Sam lock eyes. A silence stretches between them. Why is Daisy doing this to her own husband, throwing him to the wolves? She isn't making any sense.

'OK,' she says. 'I'll tell them if you won't. Sam told you some of the truth but he omitted rather a lot from his statement. The meeting with Hannah he told you about was not the last time he saw her but the time *before* last. The last time was actually the day she disappeared, when he—'

'That's not true,' Sam says, his jaw locked, body rigid. He's standing in the middle of the circle, appeals to us one by one as he looks from one face to the next. 'Don't listen to her.'

Daisy's eyes are glassy, fixed on the wall ahead, and she carries on as if he hasn't spoken.

'The last time was actually the day she disappeared, when he abducted Hannah in his van and killed her.'

Somebody gasps. *What?* I'm unable to move or take my eyes off Daisy.

'Don't listen to her.' Sam's fists are curled at his sides and his face is white. 'I loved Hannah, I would never hurt her.'

'That's not true. Another of your lies. He picked her up in his van and arranged for one of his mates to dump it somewhere later, some guy that owed him a favour. Always calling in favours is Sam. Even with his wife. More like blackmail is what I'd call it. All that stuff about the hidden admirer; he made that up, it just wasn't true.'

'But it was,' Amy said. 'Kat explained all that.'

'I don't mean Kat. Sam was hassling her; that's who the mystery someone was.'

'This is crap, guys,' Sam says. A blush creeps up his neck and veins bulge on the side of his forehead. His voice is loud and I'm not the only one who flinches. Jade's hand creeps towards Kat's. Amy flashes me a concerned look: *what the hell is going on here?* I shake my head without taking my eyes away from the sparring match that is going on in the middle of the room, supposedly the scene of a celebratory reunion. Hannah's eyes gaze down from the mantelpiece, and I want to knock the frame down, blow the tea lights out and undo the last two days.

'You win, Daisy. I swore I'd never break the promise I made to you, but you've broken your side of the bargain so I've got nothing to lose.' The blush is now covering Sam's face, and sweat beads on his forehead. 'Yes, I'll admit, I lied about the van, but only to protect you.' Saliva sprays from his mouth towards Daisy, and she curls her lip in a sneer and flinches in exaggerated fashion.

'Don't listen to him,' she says.

'Daisy took the van. She was the one driving it that day, and the one who arranged for it to be trashed. And if you don't believe me, I've got the insurance documents to prove it.'

'You haven't,' Daisy says. 'It was years ago. Why would you have kept them?'

'In case it came to this. I always knew you would turn on me one day. They prove you were added to my insurance just a few days before Hannah disappeared.'

'You never trusted me,' she says. 'All this time and I never doubted you once.'

'You never put our relationship first. You've been cheating on me. It was Theo this time, but so many others went before him. Bet your so-called friends don't know that. Why do you think I made you leave that meal early, that time with Lou and Theo? Because I could see he was exactly your type. I wanted to warn Lou, but we'd made a deal, hadn't we? A deal where we will never betray one another. Until now. Does Theo know he's just another daisy in the chain? Ha! Good joke, that.' He looks wild, his eyes darting around to look at our open-mouthed faces. He indicates us all with a grand sweep of his arm. 'Look at them; they don't know what's going on. You owe them that much. Why don't you tell them what really happened the last time *you* saw Hannah?'

Daisy moves fast, propels herself up from the sofa and lunges at him. Kat bars her way.

'Calm down, Daisy, that isn't going to help anyone. Tell us what the fuck is going on. Tell her, Amy.'

Amy's face has lost its colour and she looks to me for reassurance. I nod.

'Yes,' she says. 'You'd better tell us what Sam is talking about.'

Kat pushes Daisy gently but firmly back onto the sofa.

'Come on, Daisy. You owe it to us all.'

'Get Theo down here. I won't say anything without him.'

My stomach twists with anger. Amy nudges me, an urgent prod. 'Do as she says.'

They're still having an affair

I charge up the stairs, heart pumping. Theo is standing in our bedroom looking out into the night sky. He jumps when I enter the room but doesn't turn around. He can see my reflection in the window.

'Something has happened. It's to do with Hannah. You need to come downstairs.'

'What about us?'

'I can't think about that now. What's happening downstairs is more important.'

He looks baffled. 'What can possibly be more important than our relationship? Is this a roundabout way of telling me we're over and you can't be bothered to discuss it with me?'

'I don't owe you anything, Theo. We can talk later, but right now, something is happening and I'm scared. Please, trust me and come downstairs.' Best not to mention Daisy. She'll kick off if he doesn't come with me. A shiver runs down my spine. I'm afraid of her. If I tell Theo what she's capable of, there's no knowing what she'll do.

'What is it? What's happening?'

'Make sure you have your phone with you. I left mine on the side downstairs and I might not be able to get to it.'

'If you're that scared, let's call for help now.'

'No, I might be wrong.' I tug on his sleeve. 'Please, Theo, come with me now.'

We join the others. Kat is still standing over Daisy.

'Right, everyone's here. Let's go for a second take on that truth or dare question. But this time, Daisy, you owe it to all of us to tell the truth.'

CHAPTER TWENTY-SEVEN
Daisy

The morning began with a spell of nausea, and I knew. Knew what I'd suspected for the last two weeks and could no longer avoid. It was 6 a.m. and there was no chance of anybody being up at this ungodly hour, so I took the test down to the bathroom and locked myself in. Ten minutes later I'd chewed my nails to bits and my suspicions were confirmed. I was pregnant.

It could have been worse. If it had happened in my first year, it could have ruined my carefully laid plans, but it was almost time for finals and I'd have left by the time the baby came. The baby. A small version of Sam. Already I was assuming I'd have it, and I felt a surge of joy followed by a lurch of fear. What would Sam say?

I planned to tell him that afternoon, after our lecture. I was nervous getting ready, my fumbling fingers dropping the mascara more than once. Not only did I want to look my best for Sam, but I wasn't sure what reaction I'd get from Amy.

Ordinarily I sat with Amy in the lecture hall, but Sam had got there first so I sat with him and his friends. I saw Amy come in out of the corner of my eye, but I pretended not to. I wasn't sure how she felt about it all, what with Hannah making such a fuss. The elastic band of our friendship was stretched to the point of snapping and I didn't want to pull it any further.

The lecture finished at two and I asked Sam to come back to my room so that we could talk. Of course he thought I had an ulterior motive, and while that might well have been on the cards, I planned to tell him about the pregnancy straight away. Part of me hoped it would secure him to me; it would be a tie between us that he didn't share with Hannah. One that had a future. Already my mind was off and away making plans for post-university, assuming he was on side with me.

Amy had gone by the time we were ready to leave, so I didn't have to manage any awkward encounters, and we walked back through town with Brian and Tom. They went ahead of us so I took Sam's hand and he gave me one of his glorious smiles. His smile kicked off one of my own, and as I turned my head I locked eyes with Louise, who was on the adjacent path coming towards us with Hannah. Another friendship stretched to breaking point. She tried to divert Hannah's attention. I squeezed Sam's hand harder. Louise wasn't quick enough, though, and Hannah spotted us, before quickly turning away.

Sam dropped my hand when he saw Hannah and I shoved mine back in my pocket, ignited by a spark of fury. We were together now; why was he still bothered about her? Back at my halls, where I'd been so happy only a matter of hours earlier, everything felt wrong. Hardly any light was coming into the room, the bedding looked faded, and a musty smell hung in the air. I pushed the window open, and Sam put his arms around my waist from behind, but I pulled away.

'What's up?' he asked.

'Hannah,' I said. He shifted his gaze from me and I wanted to thump him.

'We've been over this,' he said.

'I know. But I don't believe you're one hundred per cent convinced you want to be with me.'

'What's brought this on?' His voice sounded caring, which brought a knot into my throat. Surely it was too early for my hormones to be all over the place, but something was sending my mood bouncing around like an escaped ping-pong ball.

'Just now, out there. You were holding my hand until you saw Hannah, then you dropped it. Like I was a guilty mistake. How do you think that makes me feel?'

Sam sat down on the chair by my desk. It was the only seat apart from the bed.

'It's good that you asked me back here, because we need to talk,' he said, and my insides swooped. I perched on the edge of the bed. I couldn't help putting a hand on my stomach; he couldn't be breaking up with me, could he?

'What about?'

'You go first. What did you want to say?'

I couldn't possibly reveal my secret now, not until I'd heard his version of us. The excitement I'd experienced earlier now felt like an unexploded bomb. What if he didn't want me, didn't want *us*?

'No, you. It's Hannah, isn't it?'

'Hannah is unfinished business, that's all.' He inhaled a deep breath. 'She messaged me.'

'She what?'

'She wants to see me and I agreed.'

'Did she say why?' My voice was icy.

'Not exactly, but I owe it to her to end things properly.'

'So … you're not finishing with me?'

'Of course not. I can't get you out of my mind. All through that lecture I couldn't concentrate because I kept getting a waft of your perfume. It does things to me. *You* do things to me. It's like a drug.'

I closed my eyes momentarily. It was going to be OK.

'Do you think we have a future?'

'It's way too early for that, Daisy. Let's not get too heavy about this. You know I think you're gorgeous; Christ, I can't keep my hands off you. Let's just see what happens. But I want to speak to Hannah. I'm not going behind your back; I'm telling you because we need to be able to trust one another. She's hurting, I can tell just by looking at her, and I owe it to her to give her a proper explanation. She's fragile and I'm worried about her. Can you understand that?'

Hannah's face floated into my mind. Her perfect cheekbones and translucent skin, the glossy hair that hung halfway down her back. Those eyes that had bewitched Sam for so long. I saw the way he looked at her, taking in her willowy figure in her well-fitting jeans. She was one of those sickening people who were naturally thin – my figure had to be carefully honed. I could never be as good as her. My relationship with Sam so far was largely based on sex, but was that enough to base a future on? How could I know for sure? I wondered what Hannah was thinking right at that moment, because I knew she couldn't think of anything else either, and I wished she didn't exist.

'Of course I understand,' I said, lying, 'but let's speak to her together.' He looked confused and I rushed on, desperate to convince him. 'We need to present a united front, because everything has changed now.'

'What do you mean?'

'The reason I invited you back here today. I've got important news, Sam, I'm so excited.'

'What is it?'

I reached towards the waste-paper basket and extracted the box from the pregnancy kit, discarded this morning. I held it up and he frowned.

'You're not, you can't be.'

I held my breath, eyes riveted to his face, needing to see his true feelings. For a second I thought the worst, couldn't breathe. Then his mouth twitched and broke into a smile, and I breathed again. 'Oh no, that's brilliant, but also terrible … oh no, I don't know …'

Sam's smiles were infectious. We grinned at each other like chimpanzees, then he held his arms out and we hugged each other and rolled onto the bed.

'Now do you get it?' I whispered into his ear as his hands snaked under my jumper and over my back. 'Let's tell Hannah together. Then she'll understand.'

Everything was going to be all right.

Sam arranged to meet Hannah the following day, outside the arts block. He didn't mention that I was going to be there, because we both knew she wouldn't come if she knew. The night before, I stayed over in his room, but I woke up after a couple of hours and couldn't sleep. A doubt had crept into my head and I couldn't get rid of it. What if I hadn't been pregnant? Would Sam have stood by me then? Every time I saw him, we ended up in bed. Was there enough substance in our relationship to last beyond this phase?

Most guys would have been turned off by the pregnancy, but I'd known Sam wouldn't be. He'd gone on about children ever since I'd known him. Amy used to tease him that he'd be the first of us to start a family. Thinking about Amy made me hurt. I missed her and Louise and Kat, our little group churned up by this fallout between me and Hannah. I still wasn't sure whose side they were on, and I was determined to make it mine.

Sam was sprawled out on his back, handsome face looking peaceful, and I envied him his ability to sleep no matter what was going on. A light flashed on his bedside table. His phone. I eased myself up and out of the bed, careful not to make a noise. I picked up the phone and slipped out of the room and into the student kitchen, for once not caring about the pile of unwashed dishes stacked on the draining board.

I didn't put the light on, but pulled a chair over to the window, where a street lamp cast light into the empty room. I typed in his PIN number, went to his messages and found Hannah's name second in his most recently contacted list. I started reading.

I want to see you.
It's difficult.
I miss you.
Me too.
Can we talk?
It's difficult.
Stop saying that.
It's the truth.
Have you stopped loving me?
You know I'll always love you.
That's not what I mean.
Can we talk? Don't mention the D word.
I told you, it's difficult.
Difficult because of her?
Difficult because if I see you I might change my mind.

That last message made me jolt my head up, and the chair shifted and squealed against the floor. Sam was all over the place. It was just as I feared: if he saw Hannah, I risked losing him. I went back to the messages to check when these had been sent. The night before last, so he didn't know about the pregnancy then. I was right – without the baby, he wouldn't want me.

That was the last text exchange between them. I paced the kitchen for what felt like hours. When I crept back into Sam's room and placed the phone back beside him, he hadn't even moved. Still dreaming away without a care in the world. A rush of power took hold of me as I stood looking down at him; I could do anything to him now and he wouldn't be able to defend himself. That knowledge made me feel powerful.

Over the rest of the night, I devised my plan. We'd go and meet Hannah together and I would make him choose between us. And if he made the wrong choice, then somebody was going to pay. But would it be him, or would it be Hannah?

Once I'd decided what to do, I was able to get back to sleep. Sam would meet Hannah after her lecture ended and I'd drive his van over and pick them up. We could go somewhere off campus where we could all talk properly and I could make Hannah understand once and for all that Sam and I were together now. And always would be, baby or no baby.

Sam was fine with the plan. I suggested we drive out to Blackwood Forest because the weather was lovely and we could easily find somewhere private. Did I know then what might happen? I can't say I did, but something was driving this need for privacy.

CHAPTER TWENTY-EIGHT

Daisy

I pulled up in the road adjacent to the arts building as arranged. I could see Sam waiting outside the block, headphones on, wearing a distinctive red cap, carrying his sports bag with his cricket bat sticking out. I'd forgotten he'd had a game this lunchtime. Every now and then he'd look around, pace up and down, then go back to the same spot. Students spilled out of the building and I lost sight of him. I nearly had a heart attack when his face appeared in my wing mirror. He was with Hannah and they had almost reached the van, so I started the engine. I waited for the agreed rap on the side of the vehicle, and the door screeched as Sam slid it open.

'We'll both get in the back,' he called to me.

'What's going on?' I heard Hannah ask.

'Hurry up, traffic warden's coming,' I said. It wasn't true, but I was getting antsy and I wanted to be off before Hannah changed her mind. It wasn't as if we were kidnapping her. A conversation was needed, that was all.

A hint of sickly floral fragrance entered the van as Hannah climbed in, long hair falling over her face, and my pulse sped up. The smell made me want to puke.

'Where are we going?' Hannah asked.

'Blackwood Forest,' I told her, watching her in the rear-view mirror. Her face was drawn and she'd lost weight since I'd last seen her. She muttered something to Sam and he replied, but their voices were too low for me to make out what they were saying.

'I can't hear you,' I said. A fly settled on the dashboard and I thumped it hard, obliterated it. I didn't want any more secrets to be kept from me.

Hannah winced at my harsh tone and shifted position away from Sam, looking out of the window. I recalled the texts, Sam's betrayal, and gripped the steering wheel even tighter.

'There's nothing to worry about,' I said.

She didn't react, her gaze fixed on the world outside, which sped past as I drove fast, too fast, anxious to get to our destination.

The car park at the woods was almost empty, and I parked in the nearest spot. The sun had gone in and the sky was dark, brooding. I pulled my hoodie around me, put the hood up as I got out of the car. Hannah didn't move.

'I don't get why you've brought me here. I don't want to talk to her.' She'd lowered her voice but the words sailed out of the window into my ears. I didn't want to talk to her either, but it was necessary.

I rapped my knuckles on the roof.

'Come on, it looks like rain.'

'Which is why I don't understand why we had to come here,' Hannah said as she got out of the car and slammed the door. She held her cotton jacket around herself, faking a shiver. It wasn't that cold. Sam jumped out too. His phone slid out of his pocket onto the floor of the van. I knocked it out of sight under the seat before locking the doors.

'Are you sure this is a good idea?' he said to me as Hannah wandered away from us.

'Yes, come on. We don't want to lose her.'

'But …' He held up his bag. 'Let me put this back in the van.'

'I've locked the doors. Just bring it with you. Hannah, wait up.'

'Let's get this over with,' she called back.

'OK,' I said. 'There's a clearing there, look, we can sit on that log. Come on, Sam.' I reached for his hand, but he pulled it away. His rejection stung. I thought about the texts again.

Hannah hovered by the log, only sitting down when Sam did so first. He dropped his bag on the floor next to him, then pulled out his cricket bat and drew patterns in the soil, creating little puffs of grey around their feet.

'What's so important that you had to drag me out here?' she said. 'I'm not comfortable with this at all. You've changed, Sam, since you got mixed up with her.'

'I have a name,' I said.

She shrugged.

'I wanted you both here to tell you where we stand,' I continued. 'Sam has been a bit confused lately.' Hannah flashed a glance at him. 'It's OK, I know about the texts, Sam told me. How you still want to be with him. How you think he still wants to be with you. But you've got it wrong.

'You see, what he hasn't told you is that I'm pregnant. We're having a baby, me and Sam. We're planning a life together after university.'

'But—'

I stopped him with a look. 'Whereas you, Hannah, will be going off with your first-class degree and leaving us all behind.'

'You haven't told her your plans, have you, Sam? She doesn't know about your master's.'

What master's?

'Tell her, Sam,' I said.

Sam didn't even look at me, which was infuriating; he was still poking the bat around in the ground.

'Tell her,' I repeated, and grabbed the bat from his hand. He jumped to his feet.

'This is crazy. What are we doing? I'm so sorry, Hannah, for dragging you out here. Let's go back to the van.'

'Not until you tell her you're finished with her.'

He shook his head. Hannah was still perched on the log, her face ashen.

'No,' he said. 'This isn't right.'

'*Difficult*, Sam? Is that the right word?' I jabbed the bat at the ground. 'Difficult, eh?'

Sam glared at me.

'Do you know what happened last night, Hannah? Sam was fast asleep – he looks so angelic when he sleeps, but you probably know that, don't you? Lying on his back, dead to the world. And I had a feeling even then that he was keeping secrets from me. So I took his phone, went to the kitchen and read through his messages. Messages from you, hounding him, begging him to stay with you. Pathetic it was, pathetic. That's why I had to be here when he tells you for good that he's chosen me and you should leave him alone.'

Hannah got up. A bird screeched and flew through the air.

'I'm going back to campus,' she said. 'And I'm going to report you to the campus police for threatening behaviour. This is madness. I'm surprised at you, Sam, for going along with it.'

'I'm sorry,' he said. 'I'll give you a lift. Give me the keys, Daisy.'

'What?'

'You didn't look at Sam's phone this morning, did you?' Hannah said. 'The text he sent me saying he'd made up his mind and wanted to be with me? I don't think you know him very well after all. He told me about the baby, how he feels trapped.'

'Liar.'

She glared at me, a smirk on her face, her chin held high, as if she'd won a battle. Despite my words, I knew Hannah didn't tell lies. She hadn't got it in her. Which meant she was telling the truth.

'Don't you dare turn away from me.' A twig crackled under her feet as she stepped away, and my temper snapped. I lunged at her with the bat and whacked her across the back of the head. I had to stop her leaving, leaving with my Sam. The cry she gave didn't sound human, and Sam was shouting and dropping to the ground, and I couldn't believe how much blood there was dripping from the bat.

CHAPTER TWENTY-NINE

Sam groans, clutching his head. We're all transfixed by Daisy's account. The air is thick with the horror of her words.

'Is that what happened, Sam?' Amy asks.

'Daisy swung that bat in a stupid fit of temper. Not only did I lose Hannah, but she ruined our lives,' he says. He won't look at us and his words are muffled.

'Not ruined, Sam. We have two beautiful children. That's not any kind of mistake. You love them as much as I do.'

Now he looks at Daisy. 'Of course I do, but we made choices – *I* made choices – that day that changed the course of my life forever.'

'What happened then?' Amy asks, breaking the hushed silence that has settled over the rest of us as this horror story unfolds. All we need is a campfire and I'd be back at Girl Guide camp. At least then we were able to scream into the night when the spooky stories terrified us, and comforting one another made the thrills somehow delicious. Now we're all frozen, incredulous, unable to believe what's happening. Jade is holding Kat's hand as if she'll never let go.

'Daisy regretted it as soon as it had happened,' Sam says.

Daisy nods. 'You know when they say someone sees red? That's what it was like, a flash of red-hot fury and I lashed out without thinking, Hannah was on the ground and there was so much blood. I couldn't stop screaming. Sam said he'd check she was breathing before he called the ambulance, but then he said she was dead and what on earth were we going to do?'

'Daisy had been acting crazy.' Sam picks up the story. 'But we were in it together. Hannah hadn't wanted to come with us. I'd made her, said we had to save our relationship and we should hear Daisy out and then I'd tell her I'd changed my mind and was dumping her.

'Daisy would have gone to prison for the rest of her life for a moment of madness, and the chances were I would be implicated too. I was being selfish, but it was my van and my cricket bat and my love triangle. I'd never seen this side of Daisy before and I wasn't sure anyone would believe she was capable. And she was carrying our baby. I was scared of what she might do. Now that Hannah was dead, I realised I couldn't let the baby go. That was the clincher for me. You all know what I was like about wanting kids; ever since my little brother died, I'd wanted my own little boy to remember him by.

'We talked it through and decided it would be better if nobody ever knew what had happened. We had to …' He swallows hard. 'We had to fake the hanging and hide Hannah's body. I didn't want her to be found for ages, if ever, and it was pretty windy, so it would be natural for her to be camouflaged. It was getting dark by then. My uncle's tools were in the van, and we used his shovel to cover her over – there was load of debris, leaves and twigs and …' He clears his throat as if the words are stuck. 'Anyway, we covered up what we'd done by placing a rock by her head, to make it look like she'd hit her head on it when she fell. Daisy took the SIM card from her phone and we dug a hole and buried it, along with her bag. The earth was wet, as we'd had so much rain that week, and it didn't take long. Then we vowed to each other for the sake of our unborn little boy – I knew it had to be a boy – never to tell a soul what had happened.

'I thought we'd be found out. I lost my phone somewhere that night and I was sure the police would find it in the forest and arrest me. That last term was torture. Every day I was convinced the police would turn up. By the time they did discover her body, I'd almost convinced myself she would never be found. And still they didn't come for us.

'But it meant we had to stay together, no matter what. We married soon after, as you know, and then Daisy miscarried. But by then it was too late and we resolved to stay with one another.

'And we made it work, for a long time, didn't we, Daisy, when the kids were little; it was all worth it for them. Everything was about them. Telling the secret would have meant ruining their lives. They needed us and it was our duty to stick around for them. But the last few years have been torture. Guilt chewing away at my gut.'

He looks up at us, and I see the face of the young Sam I first knew, so eager to learn and to begin his university life, so full of hope. Hoping he'd overcome the death of his little brother, get through the trauma.

'Inevitably there were cracks in our marriage, I knew Daisy had been unfaithful, but she had this hold over me. We had to stay together. As soon as I heard about this reunion, I knew it was a bad idea, that ghosts would be waiting for us, the forest so close. But Daisy persuaded me, like she always does. Though not any more.'

'You're both guilty,' Kat says. 'You both deserve to be punished.'

'I didn't kill her,' Sam says. 'That was never my plan. The truth is, Hannah and I *were* going to make a go of it. I made out to Daisy it was all pretence, but it wasn't. I would have chosen Hannah over Daisy and she robbed me of that. If it wasn't for Daisy, I'd never even have been there, and Hannah wouldn't have died.'

Daisy is staring at him coldly.

'You're lying,' she says. 'You're equally guilty. You lured her there, you told me you wanted to get rid of her. I was only going along with your instructions.'

'You bloody liar.' Sweat pools on Sam's forehead.

'You're just saying what you know they all want to hear – Hannah's bloody fangirls. You wouldn't have left me, not when I was pregnant. You wanted that baby more than I did.'

'You don't know me. Hannah was the only one who ever understood what I was really like. Maybe it's better that it's out in the open.'

'Oh, Sam,' Daisy says. 'You think I didn't know you were going to double-cross me? I was always one step ahead of you. You dropped your phone in the van and I took it to check whether you were telling me the truth. It was all there, all your lies. I buried it in the woods near Hannah.'

Sam hangs his head.

'You're as much to blame, Sam; you were there,' Kat says.

'Of course he's to blame,' Daisy agrees. 'He had a hold over me; it was only much later that I could see how he'd manipulated me.'

'You've got me all wrong. I loved Hannah.'

'Not as much as I did.' Kat lunges forward and pushes her hands against his chest. Jade pulls her back, holds her to stop her shaking.

'We should call the police,' Amy says.

'No.' Daisy's voice is icy cold. Is this the voice Hannah heard in those terrible last hours of her life? 'You promised we'd *never* go to the police, Sam. I won't let you break that promise. If you do, I'll tell them how it was your idea to fake a hanging; you were the one who brought the rope with you, after all. You helped get her up into the tree – I could never have done that by myself. You're in this too deep to dig yourself out. So nobody calls the police. None of you, do you hear me? I won't let you.'

She reaches to the mantelpiece and swipes Hannah's photo off, and there is a cracking sound as the glass smashes on the tiles.

'I'm sick of her watching me all the time. She does that anyway; she's always been stuck in my head. I don't need to see her perfect face on display.' She stands, agitated, one hand holding the table for balance. She's looking round at all of us, her eyes flicking from side to side.

Behind her, Amy looks at Jade, and Jade tugs at Kat's hand. Daisy's eyes flicker to the knife I used to cut up the cocktail fruit. Kat lunges forward to grab it, but Daisy beats her to it. She points the knife at Kat.

'Nobody goes to the police.'

'It's over, Daisy,' Kat says.

Daisy screams and hurls herself forward.

CHAPTER THIRTY

Theo throws himself against Daisy and crashes into her side, winding her. She falls against the sofa, but doesn't let go of her grip on the knife. Theo sinks into the sofa cushions behind her and Kat attempts to kick the knife from Daisy's hand, but Daisy slashes at her and cuts her leg through her trousers. Theo jumps on her again. This time she falls face down on the floor and Jade kicks the knife from her hand and away from her. Theo sits on Daisy's back. She writhes and kicks and yells. 'Stop struggling,' he says. 'It's over.'

Daisy screams, then her body goes limp. Music is still playing in the background and we're all standing like musical statues, not daring to move, stunned by the sequence of events that has just played out before us.

Sam has collapsed to the floor and has his head in his hands. Amy goes into the hall, speaking into her phone.

'Police,' she says, and gives them the address and the details.

'They're on their way,' she says, coming back into the room.

'He's trying to set me up. Stop lying to them, Sam, tell the truth. Get off me, Theo!' Daisy tries to kick Theo by flexing her knee, but the blow glances off him.

'Save your energy,' he says.

'I thought I could trust you, of all people.'

'It's over. I told you last month and I told you again earlier tonight. And I'll keep telling you. After what I've heard tonight, do you really expect me to want anything to do with you? You killed a young woman with her life ahead of her all because you couldn't control your temper.'

'It's not how he said.' Daisy's words are muffled against the rug. None of us move. Adrenaline is racing through my body. Theo has her trapped, but what about Sam? 'How could you do this to me, Sam? Only last week you said you loved me and that you'd stay with me.'

He lifts his head.

'I lied, Daisy. You frighten me, you always have. You're a psychopath, the things you've done, the way you behave. Maybe once you're locked up they'll give you some proper treatment. But I'm glad you're going to be put away for a very long time. I won't let you near our children ever again.'

'No, not the children. I won't let you.' Daisy twists, trying to throw Theo off. He holds firm.

'Isn't it time you told Sam the truth about the miscarriage?' I say, unable to bear the secret any longer.

'Don't you dare,' Daisy hisses.

'What do you mean?' Sam says.

'There was no miscarriage; she had an abortion.'

'How do you know?'

'I found out accidentally; I had a hospital appointment back in Blackwood and I ran into her at the hospital. Believe me, I wish I'd never known. It's haunted me ever since – it's why it was so hard to spend time with you. It wasn't just about what happened with Hannah.'

'Why didn't you tell me?' Sam looks at me, his face chalky white.

I shrug, lost for words. He lunges towards Daisy, but Kat stops him.

'Leave it. She can't hurt you any more.'

'Why, Daisy? Why would you do that? After everything we risked?'

'To punish you, of course. You chose her. You didn't want me, you only wanted the baby.' Her face crumples and she's crying, fat tears on her cheeks. 'And I've hated myself ever since. That's why I'll never let you take our boys.'

'How long did the police say they'd be?' Kat asks.

'Ten minutes,' Amy says.

I have no idea how long it's been. It feels as if we've been standing here forever. Hannah's framed photo lies on the floor, a large crack across her face. I look away.

Daisy writhes around again. 'Get off me. I'll report you for assault. The police won't believe a word Sam says. I'll prove to them this is a set-up, you've all got it in for me.'

The sound of a siren breaks into the air and Jade rushes to the front door. The siren becomes deafening and a car squeals to a halt. Doors slam and then everything comes to life. Two policemen enter the room, radios crackling, and take in the scene. Amy fills them in on what's happened. Theo gets up and a policeman handcuffs Daisy. Her face is streaked with mascara.

'He's the one you want, him on the floor there. He killed Hannah.'

'We're taking you both in,' the policeman says. 'The rest of you will be required to give statements.'

Daisy ignores him. 'And *he* assaulted me.' She nods at Theo. 'You hurt me,' she says to him. 'How could you take their side?' She laughs, a chilling sound. 'I know what you're doing. This is all an act, to fool her.' She looks at me. 'Did he tell you he'd booked a little place for you to stay tomorrow night? Just the two of you? Did you believe him?'

My legs feel unsteady, and I grab hold of the armchair.

'He was taking me,' she says. 'We're getting away from you all, for good.'

The policeman holding her arm leads her out of the room, and Sam follows. Just before she steps through the front door, she calls back over her shoulder.

'None of you know what happened here,' she says. 'None of you know what really happened tonight.'

'Move,' the policeman says. 'You'll have your say at the station.'

As he places his hand on top of her head and guides her into the car, she shouts through the window.

'Truth or dare. It was a great idea, wasn't it? Why don't you ask Kat why she suggested it?'

CHAPTER THIRTY-ONE
Three months later

Theo doesn't make the journey to Oxford; he's got an appointment with the estate agent and he's anxious to get a completion date sorted. Since that weekend we've made huge strides in our partnership, and the news I found out today solidifies this. I can't stop smiling; it's been that way ever since I found out a couple of hours ago. I settle into the corner seat on the train, and set my coffee and book on the table, even though I won't read a word on this journey. The story I've been telling myself for so long is coming true, and I want to savour it, revel in every detail. I don't even mind when a woman sits down opposite me. Instead of the irritation I would normally feel at this encroachment into my space, I smile at her and she gives me a warm smile back.

Amy is glowing too when she picks me up at the station. Her embrace is warm and her hair shines in the sunlight. She has an assurance that evaporated somewhat amongst the months of illness, but it's back and her skin blooms with health.

'Kat and Jade are meeting us there,' she says, unlocking her car, putting my case in the boot. I hold on to the flowers, not wanting them to get squashed.

'They're beautiful,' she says, as she starts the ignition. Music plays and I settle back into my seat, the leather sighing as I take in the station front and the row of houses across the road as if for the first time. It *is* the first time, in a way. I have a new perspective on Blackwood – it no longer holds any fear for me, and what we are about to do will seal that in my mind.

'What's it like living in the cottage?' I ask as she drives out of town towards the church, breeze tickling my skin through the window, making me feel alive, hands covering my stomach, my precious discovery.

'I've only just moved in. I rented a place while I had the cottage completely gutted and had a new kitchen and bathroom put in. I'm overseeing the decoration; my nephew is helping me – he's a trainee decorator, so it's good experience for him. And I'd rather have someone I know around. That's why you can't stay over at the moment, but we'll go back for a meal after and you can see for yourself. Kat and Jade will be coming too.'

'I can't wait.' Not staying over suits me; the events of that weekend are too fresh in my mind, so baby steps are the best way to approach this. It's the first time we've all seen each other since. I think back to the moment when the police took Sam and Daisy away, leaving the rest of us stunned. We stayed up the whole night, going over everything, looking for clues we'd missed, for signs.

Kat came clean about the game.

'Daisy put me up to it. I totally fell for it. We all knew Amy wanted to remember Hannah that night, and Daisy suggested coming out with the question in a truth or dare game. She said Amy would never go for something so blatant, but if it came from me, she might agree. She said if it was her idea, everyone would think she was being cruel, vindictive towards Hannah. That's why I was hitting the bottle hard – as well as all the stuff with Jade, I wasn't convinced about the game. But Amy seemed OK with it, and … you know the rest.'

'So she planned to set Sam up all along?' Amy asked.

'But she risked exposing herself.' I couldn't believe she'd be that brazen.

'She suspected Sam was about to drop her in it. And there's no point trying to understand it. That's Daisy all over – she likes to live on the edge,' Kat said.

Theo left early the morning after, saying he'd move back to his flat temporarily while I worked out what I wanted to do. Daisy's lies about the night in the hotel hadn't fooled me for long. It wasn't true what she said about Theo planning to go away with her. It was another of her delusions.

'Take as long as you need,' he said. 'I understand if you want out.'

It took me two weeks to make up my mind. I went back to see the counsellor – on my own this time – and I've been seeing her once a week ever since. Going over everything that has happened is helping me change the perspective and learn to lessen the guilt I've always felt about Hannah. It's not something that will happen quickly, but I'm taking my time to process everything. Theo and I have been through a lot together and I've been able to forgive him. Daisy has a ruthless streak when she wants something; unfortunately I didn't realise exactly how ruthless she could be.

Sam was right about her mental health. I'm not sure she deserves the label of psychopath – I don't know enough about that particular illness – but there is definitely something not right with her. There's no way of proving she was lying, and I have to believe Theo when he said they were finished; them getting back together was all fantasy on her part. Like the fantasy about Sam still being devoted to her. His love died a long time ago, and his fear of her was real.

Theo moved back in last month and we had a whirlwind week of house viewings, settling on the perfect little cottage in a village not far from Blackwood. Amy will almost be a neighbour. I can't wait to share my news with her.

'What are you smiling about?' she asks.

'Lots of things,' I say, 'but mostly because I've just found out I'm pregnant.'

We hug long and hard when we get out of the car, leaving it parked in the church car park. Kat and Jade are already in the restaurant, at the table Amy has reserved: four women meeting, only it's a different four this time. That old foursome has gone forever. Daisy is in custody awaiting trial, along with Sam, who faces a lesser charge. Sam's parents are looking after the children.

'A date has been set for the trial,' Kat says. 'It's going to be in November.'

'I wonder what she'll get?' I say.

'Years in prison, hopefully. Less for Sam, I imagine. No doubt we'll all be called as witnesses.'

After lunch, we stop at the florist's and the others choose flowers to take to the churchyard. They opt for bright colours, yellows and oranges, sunshine colours for Hannah. I collect my own bouquet from the car and we head towards the garden behind the church, where Hannah rests. It's close to her parents' home.

'Have you visited before?' Jade asks Amy. She's holding Kat's hand and they give each other little looks and smiles every now and then. I'm so pleased it's working out for them.

'Once,' Amy says. 'It's over there, in the corner.'

The headstone is marble, the wording simple. Hannah's parents made sure the word *friend* was included.

HANNAH ROBINSON
BELOVED DAUGHTER, SISTER, FRIEND
1984–2005

Amy arranges the flowers on the small plot and we stand in a horseshoe formation around our friend, holding hands in silence. A tiny bird flutters down to land on the headstone, its head twitching, a song spilling from its beak, before it soars off into the sky, to freedom.

CHAPTER THIRTY-TWO
Daisy

They send me to see her every Wednesday. Four on the dot, room B37. It makes a change from my cell. She has a window, barred, obviously, but the outside world is visible, and across the lawn the leaves of a willow tree hang like a curtain, the way Hannah's hair used to hang almost to her waist. The wind gusts and I imagine the swishing noise blowing through the fronds. It sends chills through my body.

I look forward to these sessions. Every Wednesday, when I brush my hair and clean my teeth in front of the tiny mirror I keep secreted inside my sock, I know that another person will look at me today, will pay attention to me, will listen to what I have to say. And I decide which story I want to tell.

Today I decide on the true version. The question that hides behind all questions, the truth they all want to get at.

Why did you kill Hannah?

Hannah had to be removed because she was in the way. I had a vision for my life and it involved Sam. Instead of sloping away quietly, like this supposedly meek girl should have done, she was digging her heels in, making a fuss. She was dangerous and she had to be obliterated. Murder wasn't my original intention that day, when we took her in the van for a little chat. I planned to give her the opportunity to walk away. But she resisted, and it cost her her life.

My affair with Theo was also unplanned. Louise had never forgiven me or Sam for falling in love, and when I met Theo, the idea came to me and I knew how to exact the perfect revenge. When I'm determined, men find it hard not to give in to me. My skills were a bit rusty, but I soon found their weak spot, the one all couples have, and I rubbed at it like a stubborn stain until he caved in. She wanted a child, you see; she was one of those women whose biological urges have the potential to drive them insane, who will follow any path, pay any amount of money to satisfy them. I know how that feels. But he didn't. I saw his hesitation, and it was enough. I worked on his weakness and he fell into my arms. I had no intention of running off with him, that night in Amy's cottage, but I couldn't resist one last little dig.

Sam and I argued the night I met Theo, a vicious argument. I almost told him the truth about the miscarriage. Having an abortion was a way of punishing him. We were married by then but I couldn't get over the fact that he *was* leaving me for her, and for that I'd never forgive him. Louise finding out was unfortunate – if only just one of us had organised transferring our records to the local hospital instead of going back – and I had to keep her on side so that I could trust her never to tell my secret to Sam. Bumping into her at the hospital was the worst thing that could have happened; I was sick and desperate and I couldn't hide the truth from her in my vulnerable state. But Louise was always the loyal one, and to be fair, she kept it quiet until it didn't matter anyway.

We argued as soon as we left the restaurant. Seeing Louise had brought it all back again, brought Hannah back, and the terror of Sam finding out about the baby. Whisky was drunk and words were flung. Cruel, terrible words.

'When we took Hannah to the woods and I saw you wanted to hurt her, I knew I'd made a terrible mistake,' he said. 'I loved Hannah and nothing else mattered. If only I'd acted faster and got her out of there. Instead I've been bound to you like a prisoner. I never loved you.'

That's why I sent an anonymous note to the police, telling them where to look for the phone. I knew it was only a matter of time before he turned on me; I wanted to get in first. Playing truth or dare was my way of exposing him to the others; they were supposed to take my side. I won't forgive them for that.

Theo was unimportant, a mere pawn in my game.

It was only ever about Sam.

A LETTER FROM LESLEY

Thank you so much for reading *The Birthday Weekend*. I hope you enjoyed reading it as much as I enjoyed writing it. If you did enjoy it, and want to keep up to date with the latest news on my new releases, just click on the link below to sign up for a newsletter. You can unsubscribe at any time and your email address will never be shared with anyone else.

www.bookouture.com/lesley-sanderson

As with my first four books, *The Orchid Girls*, *The Woman at 46 Heath Street*, *The Leaving Party* and *I Know You Lied*, I hoped to create an evocative novel about obsession, secrets and the blurred lines between love and lies. Writing *The Birthday Weekend* brought back many memories from my time at Warwick University.

If you enjoyed *The Birthday Weekend*, I would love it if you could write a short review. Getting reviews from readers who have enjoyed my writing is my favourite way to persuade other readers to pick up one of my books for the first time.

I'd also love to hear from you via social media.

Thanks again for reading,
Lesley

lsandersonbooks

@LSandersonbooks

www.lesleysanderson.com

@lesleysandersonauthor

ACKNOWLEDGEMENTS

This book was primarily written in lockdown, and getting engrossed in the story helped me through it and gave me a much-needed focus.

So many people have helped me along the way with *The Birthday Weekend.*

Thanks to the lovely people of the Lucy Cavendish Fiction Prize for shortlisting me for the 2017 prize, for the kindness of everyone involved with the event and the continued support.

To my lovely agent Hayley Steed and to everyone else at the fabulous Madeleine Milburn agency: Hayley, your continued belief in me means the world and I love your energy and enthusiasm.

To Louise Beere, thanks for the lovely chats and Yorkshire writing wisdom, and to Vikki Patis, Rona Halsall, Ruth Heald and Katie Godman for constant support and critiques.

To my lovely editor, Therese Keating – it's been great working with you on this book, and I hope there will be many more to come. To everyone at Bookouture – especially Alex, Kim, Sarah and Noelle – you all work tirelessly and with infectious enthusiasm for your authors and I'm so proud to be one of them.

To everyone at Elizabeth Garrett Anderson School, for giving me so much support and promotion for my writing.

And to everyone else – all the other writers I've met along the way, too many to name but nonetheless important – I'm so happy to be one of such a friendly group of people.

To my family, to my friends old and new for believing in me, thank you.

And of course, to Paul.

Printed in Great Britain
by Amazon